D0961880

ANNIE'S ATTIC MYSTERIES®

The Map in the Attic

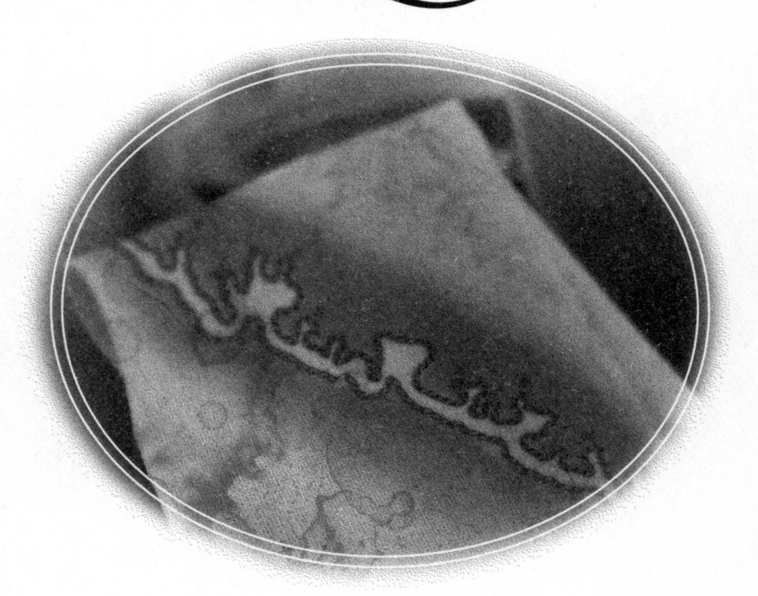

Jolyn Sharp

AnniesMysteries.com

The Map in the Attic

Library of Congress-in-Publication Data
The Map in the Attic / by Joyln Sharp
p. cm.
I. Title
2010905264

AnniesMysteries.com
800-282-6643
Annie's Attic Mysteries
Series Creator: Stenhouse & Associates, Ridgefield, Connecticut
Series Editors: Ken and Janice Tate

10 11 12 13 14 | Printed in China | 10 9 8 7 6 5 4 3

1

David Coyne sat up groggily and groped for the receiver, only to hear the dead whine of a disconnected call before it even reached his ear. It was then that his foggy brain processed the distant sound of the smoke alarm, and the acrid taste of the air. He snapped abruptly awake. Without thinking, he rolled off the bed, pulling Laura with him; she didn't wake up until her shoulder slammed to the floor. He stopped her from jumping to her feet and then pushed her in the direction of the door. The two scuttled like crabs below the smoke to the hallway. He saw her turn toward Martin's room, so he pushed along the passage to Megan's.

He felt the door for heat before pushing it open, thankful to find the smoke less dense. Megan was already awake and standing beside her bed, but when she saw her father crouched, she also dropped close to the floor. She swiftly crawled to him, and they emerged to find Martin and Laura at the top of the stairs. The parents urged their children down, following close behind.

The smoke was coming from the back of the house, under David and Laura's bedroom. The front door, which stood at the bottom of the stairs, was obscured. In that split second, David had to reason out the best course of action. He hurried them through the front door and out into the cold of an early spring night. He hoped he was the only one who turned to look back down the first-floor hall as they rushed out. Flames roiled over the living room couch and slithered up the wall of family photographs, lapping at the ceiling just beneath the spot where they had minutes ago been sleeping.

The chill, moist air only exacerbated the burning in his lungs. As they stepped into the yard, David could feel his legs weakening. But he pressed his family forward across the street before sinking to his knees and gasping uncontrollably. Through tearing eyes, he examined each member of his family; though clearly shocked and frightened, none seemed obviously injured. Laura was coughing as hard as he was, but the children clinging on either side of her helped keep her up.

With a rush, sound seemed to return to the world. The deafening roar of wood giving way under the assault of fire was cut by sirens and the shouts of neighbors, and underneath all that, the tiny sobs of Megan and Martin, just twelve and nine years old.

* * * *

"A phone call?" Bruce Besham, the fire chief of Stony Point, Maine, knew that anyone faced with a house fire was experiencing one of the most stressful events they would ever know, and he was loath to do or say anything that might make things worse. Nevertheless, he found it difficult to keep the skepticism from his voice.

David Coyne, wrapped in a blanket and now telling his story for the third time, merely nodded.

"At two in the morning?" Besham continued. Coyne merely shrugged. "And there was no one on the other end of the line?"

"They hung up," said Coyne. "Maybe it was a wrong number." Every few seconds, his eyes would scan the crowd of neighbors and firefighters, not stopping until he found his family again and assured himself they were all right. Besham didn't think he was even conscious of doing it.

Besham suppressed a sigh; this wasn't the time or the place. "Thank you, Mr. Coyne," he said. "Why don't you go have a seat in the ambulance?"

The Coynes sat in the back of the ambulance, watching the firefighters dowse the remains of their home. It was an old house, and it had burned quickly. The battle with the flames lasted several hours, and it was now almost dawn. The house was a total loss, but the houses on either side, not that close to begin with, were unharmed except for some water damage. The house had sat on a street that ran along the ocean, and the freshening breeze now mixed an incongruous whiff of salt water in with the smoke.

After the initial shock, the children had recovered quickly and were now subdued, half dozing against their mother's side. David and Laura had been treated with oxygen for their smoke inhalation and were now breathing with more comfort. The paramedics had encouraged them to go to the hospital, but the parents didn't know what they would do with the children if they'd gone, so they didn't.

David lifted his eyes beyond the remains of his house to watch the light spreading over the Atlantic out at the horizon. He knew he ought to be making a plan, figuring out where they could go to stay, how they could get clothes and other things that they would need immediately. He'd need to call the garage where he worked and tell them he wouldn't be in.

But for the moment, it was all he could do to look past the house and watch the sunrise.

After a moment he sighed and turned back to the organized chaos of hoses, firefighters, trucks, and milling neighbors. His eye was caught by the sight of an older woman in a creamy chenille housecoat and rubber boots striding purposefully toward them. In his overstimulated mind, David first thought he was seeing an angel, but then he recognized the Brock woman from down the street. David had never talked much with her, but as she approached, Laura and Megan greeted her warmly. She said some comforting words and handed David a thermos of coffee, saying she'd be right back.

He watched as she went to confer with the police chief, Reed Edwards. By the time he'd poured out some of the coffee and handed it to his wife, Miss Brock was headed back toward them. "Come on," she said briskly, "you're all coming back to my place to get some food and rest. After that, you can decide what you want to do next."

David and his wife exchanged glances and nods, but both children were already eagerly following her.

Mary Beth Brock had settled the kids in the guest room while giving David and Laura the sleeper sofa in the family room. She explained she thought it important to provide the children with something as familiar as possible. David thought that kids were pretty adaptable, but he certainly wasn't going to argue with his neighbor's kind intentions. Although the sleeper sofa was not a sterling example of the species, David assumed he would fall asleep immediately. Instead, he lay on his back listening to Laura's soft, wheezy snore and replaying the events of the evening over in his mind. How was it that the smoke alarm didn't awaken them? Who had called? Had it been a wrong number, as he'd suggested to Besham? If so, it was funny timing. No, *funny* wasn't the word for it.

Sleep, when it did come, was brief and uneasy.

Sitting at the kitchen table later that morning, a cup of coffee, and a plate of eggs and toast in front of him, David felt as if he could melt to the floor and sleep for a week. He was startled wide awake by the phone ringing again.

Mary Beth dried her hands and picked up the receiver. "Claims adjuster? We haven't called one yet, and we won't be calling you!" Mary Beth was doing a good job of fielding their calls, which had been coming at them since eight in the morning. She seemed to have a sixth sense for who was legitimate and who wasn't.

Sounds of early-morning children's TV drifted in from another room. Laura was in the bedroom with a borrowed cell phone, talking to her sister in Oregon. David smiled to himself and counted his blessings. His kids were safe, his wife was safe, he was sound, and they'd been found by a guardian angel who made great coffee.

After she hung up, Mary Beth joined him with a cup. "The fire chief wants to talk to you," she said. Her voice was measured and calm. "He wants to come over as soon as he can, but I insisted that he wait until you've had a little something to eat, and a shower. He's at your house now. Chief Edwards is with him."

David nodded as if he understood, but his mind was resisting the implications of what he was hearing.

— 2 —

Annie Dawson gave a violent sneeze.

Through watering eyes, she watched the dust motes float in the dim light of the attic, and she shivered as she pulled her cardigan close around her. The attic felt chillier in the weak springtime warmth than it did in the dead of winter. She sighed and gazed about. Sometimes the ongoing project of cleaning out the cluttered attic was an exciting treasure hunt, and sometimes it was a tedious chore; today it was the latter.

She squared her shoulders to the shelves before her; they were loaded down with innumerable boxes stuffed with who-knew-what. She ought to pick one corner of the shelves and methodically work her way through them, but she hadn't the heart. "First I'll just try to get an overall sense of what's here," she told herself, and reached out to grab a shoe box at random. It proved to be stuffed with pamphlets, old tourist maps, and other papers. And so was the next, and the next. Annie decided the shoe boxes could all wait for examination another day.

She wanted to call it quits but felt that she needed to accomplish just one more task, however trivial, before doing so. She spotted a larger box on the bottom shelf labeled "For yard sale." That would do nicely. She'd carry it downstairs, have a quick look inside, and more likely than not consign it to the fate that her grandmother had clearly once intended for it. Hefting the box, she decided it couldn't be stuffed with papers.

Annie had been steadily clearing out the attic of the old Victorian house she'd inherited from her grandmother. Betsy Holden, it turned out, had been a bit of a pack rat, but much of what she had saved had some significance. To honor her grandmother's memory, Annie felt she must treat what she found in the attic with as much care as her grandmother had. So it had been slow going.

Annie set the box down on the dining room table, enjoying the greater light and warmth of the downstairs room. The brown cardboard box was not sealed but had been closed by folding the top flaps one under another. Opening it, Annie found it was packed tightly with objects wrapped in newspaper—probably dishes. She carefully withdrew and unwrapped them, finding cups and saucers—elegant strays from someone's china set apparently; a group of five long-stemmed, tarnished silver teaspoons tied together with string; a cut-glass candy dish; a small serving platter adorned with a picture of a turkey but sized for a Cornish game hen; and other miscellaneous dishes.

Everything was lovely or interesting, but they did not constitute any sort of set. It was just a jumble of odd dishes; no wonder it had been destined for the yard sale. As Annie unpacked dish after dish, her attention started to flag. Outside, the spring sky quickly turned from light to dark to light again as clouds scudded along on brisk winds. The unsettled atmosphere brought a Gothic ambience to the rocky Maine coast, and Annie found herself beckoned by the promise of an easy chair by the fire, a cup of hot tea, and a good book.

Looking out the dining room window at the Atlantic, Annie felt a twinge of loneliness as she thought of her daughter and the twins, her five-year-old grandchildren, back home in Texas. LeeAnn and her husband Herb were still creating their home in Dallas. In Stony Point, Maine, Annie wasn't sure yet if she was disassembling her grandmother's home or creating a new home for herself. She continued unwrapping the dishes, but flashes of her own Texas life and her late husband Wayne sparked in her mind. Here in Maine, the winter's snow lingered in shadier spots, while her garden in Texas would by now be abloom.

Annie smiled distractedly as one large bundle of newspaper revealed a colorful ceramic clown. She thought it must be a cookie jar; yes, its hat was the lid, now held in place by ancient cellophane tape. But the large and oddly shaped jar was awkward to hold, and the newspaper was slippery against its smooth surface. Annie felt it slide in her hands; as she shifted her grip, she knocked aside the clown's hat. The ancient tape let go, first one piece, leaving the hat dangling for just a moment, and then the other. Without thinking, Annie took one hand from the jar to snatch in the air at the lid—and by some miracle, she caught it.

For a moment, she stood absolutely still, not even breathing as she clutched the jar in one hand and the lid in the other. Slowly she set them both on the table and then chuckled at her own foolishness: the lid probably would have been fine if it dropped, but if she'd dropped the cookie jar itself, it would have shattered. But she'd dropped neither, she told herself, and all's well that ends well.

The surprise, and the rush of adrenaline, had shocked her mind back to the present, and she paused to catch her breath, taking a closer look at the cookie jar as she did so. He really was a colorful, cheerful little fellow, and except for a small chip in the back of the hat, he was in perfect shape. She thought of her needlecraft group, the Hook and Needle Club. "I may know of a good home for you," she said to the clown, "but you'll need a bath first."

She picked up the jar and peered inside, surprised to find that someone had apparently stuffed newspaper down in there as well. As she started to pull it out, however, she realized it was not newspaper at all. Rather, it appeared to be a wadded-up rag or a piece of muslin fabric. In fact, as Annie pulled it out, she found it was quite a bit of fabric, with an intricately embroidered abstract design.

She pulled the entire wad from the jar and carefully spread it on the dining room table. The embroidered muslin was about the width of a place mat but longer, though not as long as a table runner. The edge was neatly hemmed by hand. She picked up one end and peered at the back, where someone had written a series of numbers, perhaps with a grease pencil, and had crossed out all but the last: "516, 620, 400, 537 ..."

But it was the front of the piece that took Annie's breath away. Running an irregular course from one end to the other was a gorgeous wave of color. Two crooked parallel green and blue lines made with small, precise chain stitches bisected the fabric, with irregular green circles dotting the blue side and brown teardrops pulling away from the green side. In each corner were more recognizable objects: the sun in the upper right corner and a half-moon in the upper left, while a cormorant dried its wings on a large rock in the bottom left corner, and a seal splashed in water on the right. In the curve of the seal's splash were the tiny letters YSP. Finally, in a cruder, broader stitch, someone had placed ten red Xs at points between the green and blue lines.

Annie stepped back and took in the whole piece at once. She couldn't imagine what, if anything, it represented, but the piece was so absorbing and intricate, with feather-like stitching and tiny French knots giving it texture and a three-dimensional appearance, that Annie felt she was looking at *something*. But what was it? And what did the numbers on the back mean? And what was it doing in an old cookie jar, for Pete's sake? She couldn't imagine that her grandmother had intended this for the yard sale.

Annie stood for a long time, lost in thought as she examined her odd treasure. She was finally drawn from her reverie by a warm pressure on her ankles, accompanied by soft purring. She was surprised to realize it was getting dark. "OK, Boots," she said, smiling down into the shadows at her feet, "let me put this stuff away, and then we'll see about your dinner. Sound good?" She bent down and stroked the cat.

Annie tried to rewrap the dishes carefully, but even without the cookie jar, they didn't go back into the box as readily as they'd come out. Though she was growing impatient, Annie forced herself to handle the delicate dishes with care. Finally they were back in the box, and Annie reclosed it and set it down in a corner. She carefully picked up the cookie jar and carried it off to the kitchen, Boots following expectantly at her heels.

* * * *

There was always something soothing and familiar about the smell of A Stitch in Time, the yarn shop where the Hook and Needle Club met on Tuesday mornings. It was a smell of wool and lanolin and lavender and sometimes the lingering scent of someone's perfume. Upon entering the shop, accompanied by the tinkling bell over the door, Annie often felt overwhelmed by the riot of colors and the promise of so many crocheting projects. Sometimes she would stop for a moment just inside the door to close her eyes and allow the scent to calm her mind and counteract the overstimulation of her other senses.

Fortunately, on this day there was no other customer right behind her, trying to get past her into the shop.

As she moved toward the tables at the front of the store, Annie could hear Mary Beth and Kate preparing for the arrival of the club's members, but her view of the two women was blocked by a new display of Two Ewe yarn. Two Ewe, Annie read on a handprinted poster next to the display, had started out as a sheep farm about fifty miles inland from Stony Point; it had subsequently morphed into a spinnery, first using their own wool and eventually experimenting with and incorporating other fibers as well. Annie reached out to feel the silk mohair on display, and an "ahhh" escaped her.

"Annie, is that you?" Mary Beth Brock hollered from the back of the room. "You're the first one here today."

"Oh, Mary Beth," Annie said, holding one of the skeins of yarn against her cheek, "this is heavenly."

"Don't I know it!" Mary Beth Brock was suddenly at Annie's side, smiling broadly at her response to the yarn. As the owner of A Stitch in Time, Mary Beth was always trying new lines and products in the store, and she enjoyed the responses they drew from her friends and customers.

Mary Beth's sudden appearance startled Annie, and she dropped the yarn, to Mary Beth's amusement. Still, she couldn't resist picking up the skeins again and holding them next to one another. The strands in each skein were a delicate combination of two colors—altogether there were four color combinations: sea foam and cream, fire yellow and peach, light pink and cream, and sea foam and fire yellow—with the effect of a gossamer-like "bloom."

"I was a little nervous about this line," Mary Beth continued, "but wait till you see Kate's sample. She created a simple jacket with Two Ewe's taupe cashmere yarn and then did the neckline with this—Kate! You did bring it in with you to show everyone, right?"

"I didn't forget." Kate Stevens appeared around the corner of the display with her hands wrapped around a mug of tea. She was Mary Beth's only employee and an expert crocheter. "I'm still working on the sleeves, but you can get an idea of what the finished sweater will look like."

The three women turned as the bell on the door tinkled again, announcing the arrival of Stella Brickson and Gwendolyn Palmer, followed a few minutes later by Peggy Carson and Alice MacFarlane, Annie's neighbor and closest friend in Stony Point. The new display caught their attention as well, and Mary Beth had to herd the women to their seats.

"We're stitching on a mission now," she reminded them, "so why don't we have an update on our projects? Who would like to start?"

It was Mary Beth who had brought the plight of the Coyne family to the attention of the Hook and Needle Club. Because of the fire that destroyed their home, the Coynes had moved to a temporary apartment out in the Youngstown Arms complex on the far side of town while they sorted out their situation and rebuilt. But Mary Beth, who had been in regular contact with the family, had reported to the group that the Coynes were still very stressed and despondent and just not bouncing back—especially the kids; they were picking up on their parents' anxiety, and their schoolwork was suffering. When Mary Beth had described their small, dark apartment, with dusty blinds in the windows and mouse-brown rug and furniture, the group had unanimously decided on a "color intervention" to help them settle more comfortably there.

Stella pulled from her knitting bag a stack of mitered squares in three different sizes. "I just have one more large one to do, and then we can start assembling the afghan." She passed around the squares of jewel-toned colors, which were met with admiration by all the women.

Gwendolyn and Mary Beth were knitting oversized, colorful swatches that they planned to back with felt for use as coasters and place mats, while Peggy was sewing up some cafe curtains. Alice was working on a pair of cross-stitched wall decorations from patterns that Annie's grandmother Betsy had created. Mary Beth nodded with satisfaction, remarking, "These should really brighten up the place."

In addition to her tote, Annie had brought another canvas shoulder bag, which sat on the floor by her chair. She now reached down and hoisted it onto her lap. "Speaking of things that are bright," she said as she pulled out the clown-shaped cookie jar, "I found this in my grandmother's attic. He's got a little chip on the back of his hat, but he seemed so cheerful, I wondered if the Coynes might like to have him to brighten up their kitchen."

She handed the jar to Gwendolyn, who was leaning forward to give it more scrutiny. But for a moment, nobody said anything. Suddenly embarrassed, Annie continued, "I mean, I don't want it to seem like I'm giving them castoffs …" She suddenly once again felt like the outsider in Stony Point, liable to do something inappropriate or give unintended offense.

"Annie," Mary Beth exclaimed, "it couldn't be more perfect!" Annie released a breath she hadn't realized she was holding. "Did I mention that Laura Coyne lost her collection of Fiestaware in the fire?" Mary Beth continued. "She loves those old ceramic dishes; she practically has a Ph.D. in Ohio pottery." The others quickly agreed that the jar would make an excellent complement to the needlecraft presents.

As the jar continued around the circle, their conversation turned to the "Coyne predicament," as Mary Beth called it. Even before the investigation was completed, town gossip had declared that the origin of the fire was suspicious.

"Who could suspect David Coyne of putting his own family in danger? Ridiculous!" Mary Beth fumed.

"They come in for lunch at The Cup & Saucer," Peggy said. "Or they used to; I haven't seen them since the fire." Peggy was a waitress at The Cup & Saucer, right next door to A Stitch in Time on Main Street. "But they seem very nice. I'm sure no one thinks David Coyne set fire to his own house."

"Some do think exactly that," Stella cut in, and in response to Mary Beth's stunned expression, she added, "I don't, but people are saying that Coyne was hard up and reckoned he could collect on insurance."

"Bunk!" Mary Beth nearly barked. "They cherished their old house and their deep roots in the community."

"They both certainly come from old families," Alice agreed.

It was Gwendolyn, always a peacemaker, who steered the conversation to the two children, Megan and Martin. "I hear you really have a way with them," she said to Mary Beth.

Mary Beth took a deep, calming breath and said, "They call me their *honorary* grandmother." She then described her plan to bring Megan into the Hook and Needle Club. "She has a natural eye for color, and she loves to knit! She's done some lovely scarves, but I think she's ready to advance. I'm hoping I can get her to join us during her summer break. She's a neat kid but a little shy."

"What? Afraid of a bunch of women with sharp objects in their hands?" Alice winked at Mary Beth as she passed along the cookie jar.

"Well, even so," Peggy, a quilter, said, "the family needs help. I've been in those Youngstown apartments. They're as dismal inside as out, dark and damp, and the yard's been turned into one big, dusty, parking lot."

"Well," Stella said, examining the jar critically, "this is certainly a collector's item, possibly a valuable one. You found it in Betsy's attic, you say?"

"In a box marked 'For yard sale,' with a lot of old, random china cups and saucers. Laura would be welcome to have those, too," Annie added tentatively, "if she really likes dishes." She watched Mary Beth's face carefully for a reaction but couldn't tell whether she thought this a good idea. Deciding to change the subject, Annie reached for her crochet project saying, "You won't believe what I found *inside* the cookie jar!"

"Oh, I don't want to know!" Peggy said quickly. "I had them in my attic and getting rid of them was a pain in the …"

"No, no," Annie laughed. "Nothing like that. No, someone had stuffed a beautiful piece of embroidery down inside the jar. I can't imagine why, but it's just lovely, sort of an abstract design." She tried to describe it, though she felt her attempt fell far short.

"Annie Dawson," Mary Beth interrupted her fumbling description. "You didn't bring it along to show us? For shame!" The other women laughed and encouraged her to bring the piece in.

Annie laughed with relief. "Well, of course. I should have. And I will next week. Maybe you'll be able to tell me what I'm looking at!"

— 3 —

Annie had stopped off for milk and eggs on her way home from the meeting of the Hook and Needle Club, and back at Grey Gables she made herself a tuna fish sandwich for lunch. No sooner had she washed up her dishes, however, than she heard a tapping on the glass pane of the kitchen door. She wasn't surprised to find her neighbor on the other side, and when Alice entered with a covered plate of something that smelled freshly baked, Annie immediately set a kettle of water to boil.

"This isn't a bribe, exactly," Alice said, removing the linen cloth and revealing a plate of muffins, "but these are the ginger-blueberry ones you liked so much, and I thought—"

"Alice MacFarlane! I don't believe you had time enough to do all that baking." Annie reached for two small plates and mugs that were still in the dish drainer by the sink and brought them to the table. "Do you have a magic wand or something? And if so, can I borrow it?" She turned toward the refrigerator. "Butter?"

"Umm ... I don't think these need butter. Now about that—"

"Cookie jar? Wasn't that the cutest?"

"You!" Alice laughed. "You know I'm eager to see this piece of embroidery."

"Yes, I suspected as much." Annie smiled. "Here, get

the tea and water when it boils, and I'll bring it in."

Despite the alluring aroma of the muffins, they were almost forgotten when Annie spread the embroidered muslin on the kitchen table.

Alice gasped as she smoothed out the fabric, running her fingers lightly over the undulating lines of color. "Oh my" was all she could muster for a few moments. "It looks to be, sort of, in the Arts and Crafts style, doesn't it? It reminds me of some of the Tiffany lamps I've seen and things from that era. I think it's something about the colors."

"It does," Annie agreed, "and yet it doesn't."

"Right. And these Xs are odd. They don't seem to go with the rest. I wonder if they were added later by someone who wasn't a needlecrafter? Hmmm." Alice's reaction mirrored Annie's when she first saw the embroidery. Alice was scanning the intricate patterns and finding more details in the craftsmanship and design. Alice carefully turned the muslin over and pointed to the odd numbering. "What do you think this means?"

"Not a clue. I was hoping you might have an idea ... I can't say for certain, but this doesn't strike me as something Gram did."

Alice folded the canvas gently in half, nodding in agreement. "No, it's not her style. Tell me again, where exactly did you find it?"

Annie described the box of dishes and the cookie jar. "This was just wadded up inside."

"Which makes me wonder if Betsy even knew it was in there. Annie, let's go look at the box; we may be able to tell by the newspaper wrappings when it was packed."

Annie scooped up the piece and returned it to the dining room, where she'd been keeping it in a pillowcase on the sideboard. Then she turned to the corner where she'd set the box and lifted it onto the table. Each wrapped item came out again, and they noted that the pieces had all been protected with sheets of the *Maine Sunday Telegram* for May 16, 1982. Annie had been in high school at the time.

"It seems odd that she would have packed this stuff up for sale without even looking in the jar," Annie said. "That just doesn't seem like Gram."

"No, it doesn't," Alice agreed, "but neither can I imagine her leaving that in there if she knew about it." Alice frowned at the little bundle of tarnished teaspoons. After a moment, she continued, "The thing is, Annie, do you recognize any of this stuff?" Annie gave her a questioning look. "Like the cookie jar; do you ever remember seeing it out on the kitchen counter?"

Now it was Annie's turn to frown. "No, I don't." And then illumination flooded her face. "I see what you're getting at. Gram wasn't taking this stuff *to* a yard sale. She brought it back from one." She considered this for a moment. "But why would she just put the whole box away in the attic, then?"

Alice shrugged. "I can think of any number of reasons. Maybe she bought the box just for the sake of one piece, so she removed that and put the rest away. Or maybe it was late in the day, and they threw this in with some other box that she was buying. Or maybe life just got in the way—by the time she got home, it was time to cook dinner or she had to go out, and she just never got around to looking through this." She gave a rueful smile. "To tell you the truth, Annie, any of those sound more like the Betsy I knew. It has to be admitted: She brought in a lot more stuff than she took out."

Annie laughed. "That's why I have all these treasures to sort through!" She turned her attention back to the dishware and newspapers spread out on the table. "OK, so this stuff all belonged to somebody else, and Gram picked it up in a yard sale. Clearly, she didn't know the embroidery was inside the jar, but I still think whoever packed it up must not have known either, or they wouldn't have left it in there. But it's such a beautiful piece, how could that be?"

"Well, if someone was packing up after a parent or grandparent had passed away ..." Alice raised her eyebrows and made a gesture encompassing Grey Gables. "Not everyone invests the kind of time and care you are, Annie. Some don't want to; many can't afford to."

Annie felt humbled, realizing once again that this chance to connect with her grandmother's heritage was a gift, even if at times it felt like a chore. "I guess there's no chance of finding out more about how Gram came to have it. Even if we ask around, who's going to remember whether they had a yard sale in May of 1982?"

"We don't even know that it was local," Alice said. "*The Telegram* circulates all over. Betsy might have gone out for a drive some nice day." Annie hung her head, feeling defeated.

"You should have it framed," Alice suggested after a moment. "It would look great over the sideboard here, and that wall doesn't get much sunlight so the material would be protected." When Annie didn't respond, she continued,

"Come on; let's get back to our muffins."

The two women returned to the kitchen and settled down at the table. They ate in silence for a while, until finally Annie said, "You're right, these don't need butter. Alice, I wish I knew your secret."

"Magic wand."

Annie smiled. She reached for a bag hanging on the back of one of the kitchen chairs. "I stayed behind and bought some yarn this morning."

"Is it the Two Ewe yarn?"

She nodded. "I got enough for a shawl for LeeAnn. I think I can finish it in time for her birthday, or if not, then by Christmas." Annie emptied the bag of skeins of sea foam and cream silk mohair and a one-page pattern. "I thought I would do a lacy, broad shawl. Here's the pattern Mary Beth suggested."

Alice looked at the sketch on the front of the pattern. "Very elegant. She's good with matching people to yarns and patterns, isn't she?"

Annie imagined her daughter stepping out on the town in such a shawl. She only wished she could be there to babysit the twins when LeeAnn went out.

"You know," said Alice thoughtfully. "When I spoke of framing the embroidery, it made me think how much it looks like a painting, at least to me." Annie looked at her with interest. "Who knows? Maybe it's based on a painting. Or maybe it was made by someone who worked in more than one medium. It's a long shot, but it might be a way to find out something about it. I bet Betsy had some books around here about local artists. She wasn't a stranger to the galleries and museums. Have you noticed any pamphlets or catalogs on her shelves?"

"You're right, it's a long shot," Annie said with a broad smile. "But it's a start. That will be my homework for tonight."

* * * *

Over the next several evenings, Annie searched the library of Grey Gables and rounded up a fair number of art books, including catalogs of special exhibits at the Farnsworth Museum and brochures from some of the larger galleries in the area. Paging through them, she was able to form a general overview of Maine artists and area decorative arts, but she found no paintings that resembled the style of the embroidery piece, or anything that related to embroidery styles or historical textiles.

She went to bed each night with the names of artists and images of rocky coastline buzzing in her head, but she felt frustrated and more curious than ever. The embroidery's craftsmanship suggested that it was more than a schoolgirl's primer piece, while the design and use of color possibly spoke of someone with artistic training. Annie was disappointed to find nothing in any of her grandmother's books that gave her the slightest hint about its origins.

At breakfast on Friday, she resolved to go to the public library for a more exhaustive perusal of regional art catalogs. She called Alice to see if she was free for an afternoon search. Would she be willing to help Annie out if they threw in lunch at The Cup & Saucer?

"I would love a distraction, Annie," Alice told her. "I've been making paper Barbie doll hats all morning for a party centerpiece." She laughed ruefully. "Well, it seemed like a good idea when I was drifting off to sleep last night. But now my hands hurt, and the little hats are more tacky than fun. I need a new idea, and a little fresh air will do me good." Alice was constantly designing fun centerpieces for the home parties at which she sold Princessa jewelry and Divine Décor products. When Annie had unearthed some old Barbie dolls in the attic recently, Alice had seen their potential immediately and begged Annie to sell them to her. Annie wouldn't take her money, but she accepted Alice's donation to the Volunteer Firemen's Fund in exchange.

Over lunch, Annie described for Alice what she had learned from the catalogs. "Unfortunately, Gram's stash isn't exhaustive, and it's mostly focused on fine art. My sense is that what we have would fall more comfortably under folk or decorative art."

Leaving The Cup & Saucer, the pair walked to the Stony Point Library, which was housed in a stark white building with black shutters. It was a graceful Greek-revival building, but for Annie the spare detailing characterized Old New England.

Annie and Alice paused to hash out their research plan in the library's foyer, speaking in whispers so as not to disturb the other patrons. Annie carried a canvas tote bag filled with mystery novels due to be returned. As she glanced around, she saw few open seats in the Great Room; the reference room was only moderately less crowded. For a weekday afternoon the library was fairly busy. With a wry smile she asked, "Who says reading is passé?"

Alice turned to the two computer terminals incongruously perched on an antique table. "I do miss those old card catalogs, though."

Thinking back, Annie could recall that the cabinets for the card catalog had once stood where the table did now, though they took up rather more space and had created a darker atmosphere.

"I had a game as a kid—" Alice continued, "I would pull open a drawer at random, part the cards without looking, and check out whatever book my fingers landed on. I think I was trying to be the kid with the longest list of borrowed books, but serendipity sure led me to some interesting topics."

Frustrated with her wearisome paging through art books, Annie had decided on a new approach. While Alice turned to the computerized card catalog, Annie took out a clipping from one of the newspaper sheets that had been in the box of dishes and approached Grace Emory, the reference librarian on duty.

Grace was a petite woman with boyish-cut brown hair streaked with blond highlights and piercing blue eyes. She looked over her reading glasses at Annie and then dropped her gaze to the scrap of newspaper in Annie's hand. Without speaking, she reached out to take the wrinkled clipping and raised her eyebrows questioningly at Annie.

"Ah, hello, Grace." Annie shrugged. "I wonder if the library would have old copies of *The Telegram* on microfilm." She gestured vaguely toward the paper. "I'd like to see the papers from May and June 1982."

"What are you looking for?"

"Well," Annie stammered. "Notices of rummage sales, yard sales, and the like."

Grace took off her glasses, letting them hang around her neck on a beaded chain, and stared at Annie for a moment. Then she smiled. "Now you've piqued my curiosity. What *exactly* is it you're looking for?"

Annie exhaled and spilled out the story of unpacking the box of dishes and finding the muslin fabric in the old cookie jar. Crossing her arms, Grace stared at a point on the desk in front of her as she listened, nodding occasionally.

When Annie finished, Grace said, "Two things. I can get you microfilms of *The Telegram,* and *The Point* too. Mike Malone's paper is the place where you usually see the estate sales and auction notices, and those usually carry some sort of description of the contents being sold. But if the dishes in the box were old, it's possible this piece of embroidery is older still. Have you tried the Historical Society? Or the Maine Folk Arts Center over in West Waring?" Annie shook her head. "The Folk Arts Center typically focuses on lesser-known artists, and they've had a few exhibits featuring textile artists from the area over the years. While you get settled, I'll just run down to the basement and pull those films; there's the reader over there. Then I'll get you some information about the Folk Arts Center."

Settling in front of the microfiche machine, Annie reached in her purse, pulled out a small notebook, and jotted down Grace's suggestions. *Textile artists*, she said to herself, and jotted a note to check some of the finer arts-and-crafts stores in hopes that someone there could point out something about the piece. She was intrigued to learn of the Folk Arts Center, which sounded like an interesting place to visit even if they couldn't help with the embroidery.

When Grace returned with the boxes of film, Annie fitted the spools on the spindles and threaded the film before the lens; she began slowly turning through the back issues of the newspaper. She wasn't exactly sure what she was looking for, and the sheer volume of material seemed a little overwhelming, but she printed out several pages that listed yard-sale notices for a few weeks after the time the box of dishes had been packed.

As she scanned through, her attention was caught by an article about a couple of "young people" starting their own sheep farm. In the accompanying photograph, a woman in a flannel shirt and a tall, thin young man with dark hair and a scraggly beard stood next to a hand-painted sign that read "Two Ewe Farm." She read the article that described their small herd of sheep and one female Angora goat. Annie made a printout of the article to show the Hook and Needle Club.

When Annie didn't think she could keep her eyes focused any longer, Alice's melodic voice jolted her awake—as apparently it did a few other patrons. Alice apologized and dropped her voice down to a whisper.

"I've checked out a few books on textile arts in Maine, but really, I couldn't find much on the history. Mostly it's 'how-to' books. And here—" Alice pulled from the bottom of her stack an oversized picture book. "Just because it was so beautiful, a book of photos of the Maine shoreline."

"And a few mysteries, I see," Annie added.

Alice smiled. "I got you the latest Donna Leon. They said it just came in."

The two of them moved to a table, and Annie had just started flipping through one of the oversized volumes when she was interrupted by a trio of boisterous girls who burst into the reference room, filling it with giggles. They were quickly shushed by the librarian. With a damper put on their fun, they turned around and marched back out as noisily as they had come in. As the door shut, Annie could hear a faint echo of self-absorbed, exuberant chatter. She looked around and briefly locked eyes with another girl who'd been quietly reading in an overstuffed chair. In that moment, Annie noticed her uncombed brown hair, her gray, oversized long-sleeved T-shirt and faded jeans, and her intense, unsmiling gaze.

Alice then spoke softly in Annie's ear, "Over there in the chair … that's the Coyne daughter."

— 4 —

Being thorough, Grace Emory had seen to it that Annie had all the information she needed about the Maine Folk Arts Center, including the key person to talk with, its hours of operation, and driving directions. She had also found and copied for Annie a few scholarly articles on topics such as cotton-fiber production in the Maine mills. All this, along with the mystery novels that Alice had picked out for her, left Annie with more than enough reading for the weekend, though in the end, she didn't get to much of it.

Though the weather Saturday morning wasn't quite warm enough for setting out new seedlings and transplanting plants, Annie was eager to get her hands dirty in the garden. Her errands that day included a stop at the nursery to get mulch and other gardening supplies. When she returned to Grey Gables, she noticed the crocuses were dotting the edges of the front walk, and tulips and daffodils were just starting to push up. Gazing out the kitchen window, Annie could imagine what the yard would look like when the buds finally burst out into full color.

After lunch, she donned her Windbreaker once more and stepped out into the breezy sunshine. Turning her back on her beloved view of the ocean, Annie critically surveyed the house's exterior and yard, and then took an inspection tour around the old Victorian. Her examination revealed a number of things that needed attention: a clogged gutter too high up for Annie to comfortably reach by ladder, peeling paint, and perhaps a little wood rot close to the ground. Annie sighed: With old houses—and with new—something always needed a handyman's TLC. Plus there were the usual spring-cleaning chores: raking the yard, picking up sticks, washing the windows. Though she was pushing the season a bit, Annie decided to swap out the storm windows for the screens.

That night she called Freddy Johnson, a neighborhood twelve-year-old and budding entrepreneur who was always ready to earn some cash by doing chores. Yes, he was available to come by on Sunday for some general cleaning and sprucing up. She got to work on a list.

All weekend, however, Annie's thoughts kept drifting back to the Coyne girl that she'd seen in the library—Megan, her name was. There was a lonesomeness in that look of hers, but Annie also sensed strength or stoicism. She recalled a favorite saying of her father's: "This too shall pass." Her father, a missionary, had seen a lot of trouble around the world, and yet the resourcefulness of the people he worked with constantly amazed him, he had said. Human beings soldiered on somehow in the face of tragedy. They found hope and resources to start over.

As Freddy bustled about on Sunday afternoon, sweeping the porch and washing the windows, Annie thought of asking him about Megan; they must be about the same age and perhaps knew one another from school. His cheerful animation seemed a sharp contrast to Megan's quiet seriousness, however, and Annie decided that asking about the girl would seem too much like prying: kids were always suspicious when adults started quizzing them about their peers. But though she kept her questions to herself, she couldn't get the image of the girl in the library chair out of her mind.

* * * *

Tuesday morning, Alice came over to ride with Annie to the Hook and Needle Club meeting. She had to remind Annie to bring the embroidery.

"You won't be very popular if you forget that!" Alice remarked.

"I know," Annie said, "but I've been a little distracted. I can't stop thinking about Megan Coyne." Annie placed the embroidery in a felted tote bag, a gift she had bought for herself at the Stony Point Summer Craft Fair last year. It was too small to hold groceries or large crochet projects, so Annie was pleased to find a special use for it now.

"The Coynes are going to be OK," Alice assured her. "Their luck changed the minute Mary Beth made them her special project."

Annie had prepared herself for the Hook and Needle Club by getting a head start on the crocheted shawl she'd planned to make with the Two Ewe yarn. She'd learned from experience that she couldn't focus on counting stitches or following complex directions when the group was engaged in an animated discussion. It was best to arrive with something already started.

She found the Two Ewe display reduced to half of what it had been. Settling into her usual chair and looking around at the other women's projects, Annie understood why. Half the club was making something with the gossamer yarn. The stuff must have fairly flown off the shelves during the week. Annie enjoyed the group's initial show-and-tell, and she eagerly waited her turn so she could share the newspaper article about the two kids just out of college starting their own farm. Mary Beth was ringing up a sale when Annie showed the printout around, but she was obviously keeping an ear out for what the group was saying, for they heard a resonating "my goodness" from across the store.

"But you did bring it, didn't you?" Kate asked. "The embroidery?" The other women nodded and leaned forward in anticipation.

Annie pulled out the muslin, unfolded it carefully, and spread it out across her lap so the others could see it. There was a moment of silence as it began to be passed around; then everyone spoke at once.

"Oh wow!"

"Just gorgeous!"

"What a fine hand!"

"My, my, my."

"I love the colors," Mary Beth said at last. "Very saturated, the colors of nature. Maine woods on a rainy day."

"Just wadded up, you said?" Gwendolyn reached out for the embroidery piece for a second look. "It seems an odd shape. And those red Xs—eight, nine, ten of them. They must mean something. Hmm ..."

The women were silent again as the piece made another round of the circle. Then suddenly Kate muttered, "Huh," in a tone that immediately attracted their attention. "Huh," she repeated. A slow smile of understanding spread across her face.

Looking up, she met their questioning gazes. "When I first saw it, I thought something about it was familiar," she began, relishing the suspense. "Not that I've ever seen anything like it before, but ... it rang some sort of bell."

"And?"

Kate gave a happy laugh. "It's a map! Or a kind of one, I mean. Of the coastline!" The other women frowned as they tried to apply this idea to the embroidery. "Look here, this is Caleb's Cove," Kate continued, pointing to one of the tight curves in the meandering embroidered line that bisected the fabric. "And just south is the harbor and the beach, and this gray circle—" Kate pointed to some small, tight stitches that radiated from a faint yellow French knot."— this must be the lighthouse."

The other women nodded slowly as they tried to visualize their local coastline and then project that image onto the design. Stella pulled the piece over to where she could inspect it closely. "Mary Beth, do you have a map here? A real one?"

Mary Beth didn't, but Peggy volunteered to run down the street to the library and bring one back from the rack just inside the door. While Peggy was away, Annie told the group about the librarian's suggestion of taking the embroidery to the Historical Society or the Maine Folk Arts Center. "She described a few craft *movements*, if you want to call them that, that might be chronicled more thoroughly in a museum that celebrates the local art and artists."

"Movement. You mean like a trend or something?

Interesting." Stella crossed her arms. As she thought for a moment, her eyes drifted over the cubbyholes filled with yarn. "Interesting," she said again.

Peggy was breathless when she returned with a cartoonish tourist map of Stony Point, a state road map, and a number of glossy flyers with sites to see along the coast of Maine. "The road map didn't do much justice to little ol' Stony Point, so I picked up everything they had," Peggy explained. Kate set a large plastic storage box in the center of the group, and Peggy spread the maps out on that.

It was the crude cartoon map that most clearly matched the undulating lines of the embroidered muslin. On it the major tourist attractions were highlighted on a colorful map, with business-card–sized ads framing the picture. "See, Caleb's Cove," Kate said, "which makes this next one to the north Smith Cove, and then Pemmiteck Point ..." The women crowded together over the map, continuing to name the various bays, points, and rivers. They determined that the map represented about fifty miles of coastline, about two-thirds of it to the north of Stony Point.

When they finished, it was clear how remarkably accurate the embroidery was in its depiction of the coast. "But I still don't understand what the red Xs are," Kate said after a thoughtful silence, still glancing back and forth between the embroidery and the maps. "They certainly don't correspond with the towns on shore. I suppose they might be channel markers? Or buoys?"

"Lobster traps?" Peggy put in.

The women continued to speculate about the significance of the Xs, but they were unable to come up with a satisfactory explanation. In the end, they decided the Xs most likely had something to do with fishing or lobstering. There were too few to indicate individual lobster traps, but they might represent productive beds.

"Annie, you've got to find out more about this," Kate said. "If there's a chance that Liz Booth at the Historical Society or someone at the Folk Arts Center could throw any light on this, I think you should check it out, or we'll all just die of curiosity."

Several of the women had visited the Folk Arts Center, and they provided Annie with more information about its work and location. They spoke so earnestly and gazed at her so intently that Annie started to feel a little spooked. Finally, after a particularly pregnant pause, Alice intoned, "Annie, you must accept this mission. The future of Stony Point depends on you."

Everyone laughed, and Annie said, "OK, I'll do what I can. But you," she turned to Alice, "you just may find yourself drafted to play Watson."

* * * *

On the drive back to Grey Gables, Alice said, "You've been out to Caleb's Cove, Annie, remember? The sea kayaking we did in summer day camp. What did we call ourselves?"

"The Pointer Sisters," Annie said.

"That's right. And I think we adopted a disco theme song. Do you recall what it was?"

"Sorry, no. I've repressed it, I'm sure. I do remember how scary it was to be out on the open water in the kayak, though." Their talk turned to other things, but once she was home, Annie made herself a cup of tea and sat in her living room, looking out at the ocean and thinking.

She had never really forgotten the day she and Alice and the "Pointer Sisters" made the trip to Caleb's Cove. Alice was wrong about it being camp, though. It was a church youth group, only that summer, by coincidence, there had been no boys, so the girls had called themselves the Pointer Sisters, and it stuck. They'd been learning to kayak all summer in a pool and on lakes; they had built up their boating skills and had each passed a water-safety course. The trip on the ocean was the culminating excursion, and it was exhilarating and frightening. Annie remembered being pulled out into the open sea and the calm presence of the instructor as he coached her on the finer points of controlling the kayak in the presence of waves and currents. All the way out to the cove, Annie had felt just on the edge of losing control of her craft, awkward and self-conscious in the bulky life jacket, and alternately overheated and chilled by the sun and the breeze. Once in the cove itself, the water stilled, and the group found a place to debark and break for lunch.

The beach wasn't sandy but consisted of pebbles, so the group walked farther in to a shady spot where they could spread out a couple of tablecloths and enjoy the view and gossip and torment their instructor. Annie had been enjoying the feel of the sunshine on her legs when all of a sudden a dense, threatening cloud cover blotted out the sun. The mood of the group responded immediately. The girls quieted down, becoming almost sullen. What had been dappled light under the trees became gloomy shadows. Annie could pick out little bits of trash that had washed ashore, and somewhere she heard a radio, a faint but ghostly reminder that the little cove wasn't so isolated after all.

Annie and Alice shared an extra-large beach towel as they waited for the weather to turn. In true Maine fashion, the clouds blew away, and the sun returned within minutes. But this time the sun felt harsh and glaring, and the little cove's imperfections didn't remain hidden. The rocks jutting out of the water that she had navigated around in the kayak seemed now to be larger, and more menacing. Then the wind picked up, whistling and howling as if pleading for an escape from Caleb's Cove. Annie wondered if the out-of-the-way spot was haunted.

The Pointer Sisters made good time paddling back to Stony Point's beach, and Annie was relieved to find her grandfather waiting for her. Charles Holden seemed to sense that Annie was rattled, for he suggested she wait in the car while he helped load the kayaks onto the trailer that would cart them back to the boathouse.

Safe and sound once again at Grey Gables, Annie sat with her grandfather on the porch swing and grilled him about shipwrecks off the coast and pirate ships. Charles Holden had an encyclopedic knowledge of sea lore, and he told Annie the story of the great Irish pirate Grace O'Malley.

"Did she steal stuff?" Annie asked, sipping lemonade from a tall glass.

"Aye," he said, rubbing his chin and looking out at the ocean. "Salt, wine, silks."

"Did she ever come over to America?"

"Probably not. But we have our own pirates and buccaneers to enrich our history."

"What about shipwrecks?"

"We've got those too. Good captains—and pirates—would have known the particulars of the coast, the coves and sandbars, as well as the tides and currents of the sea. But even so, nature is capricious, and the best ships didn't always navigate as nimbly as was needed."

"So the beaches might be haunted …?"

At that her grandfather laughed, and his laughter was infectious. Annie realized then that she wasn't being rational, but she enjoyed imagining what sea life was like, especially from her vantage point on dry land.

Annie recalled that day very clearly. It had been one full of lessons, some of which she only appreciated much later in life. Now sitting in front of the fire with Boots on her lap, the history lesson from her grandfather was resonating for some reason. *It must be that odd map*, she thought, *but how was that connected to pirates or shipwrecks?* "Or am I just nuts?" she said aloud to Boots, who reacted by jumping down and pouncing on a felted mouse toy.

5

The Stony Point Historical Society managed some of the exhibition space in the new Cultural Center on Main Street, where it also had a small office. As Annie entered the center and stood under an ancient Penobscot canoe that hung from the ceiling—part of a traveling exhibition on the handicrafts of Maine's native inhabitants—she was surprised to find no volunteer guide greeting her. Visitors were unusual that early in the morning, Annie knew, but her footsteps seemed to echo loudly on the wooden floor. She could hear loud voices—an argument?—drifting in from a back room as she wandered around the exhibit and read the information provided.

The Penobscot Indian basket-weaving display was particularly interesting, with examples of all sizes and purposes. Handwritten note cards fixed to the wall offered further information, but the animated conversation disrupted her concentration. Then laughter rang out, and Annie exhaled and relaxed a bit. Had her recollection of the trip to Caleb's Cove tweaked her nerves? Annie's ear picked up more subtleties of the conversation, and she realized she was hearing mostly one excited voice—a man's. Not an argument, it seemed. The loudest laughter belonged to a woman; Annie guessed it was Liz Booth, the president of the Historical Society. Annie surmised that the hidden gentleman was working hard to amuse Liz, or convince her of something.

The beautiful and functional baskets were inspiring, and Annie was almost ready to sign up for a class on basket weaving when a surprised Liz emerged from the back and greeted her.

"I'm sorry … I didn't hear you come in. We have *got* to get a cowbell or something for the door!"

"I don't mean to interrupt," Annie said, but something in Liz's manner suggested that she welcomed the interruption.

"We have an unusual exhibit—for us, that is," said Liz, gesturing toward the baskets, "because it's cosponsored with another museum. We pooled our resources and knowledge, and we've been thrilled with the results. But you're just in time to see it: the baskets are about to come down so they can travel to other area museums for the tourist season."

"It's quite informative, but actually, I'm here about something else. I have an unusual item I was hoping you could tell me about." Annie dug into her felted tote and felt the now-familiar roughness of the back of the muslin.

Liz guided Annie over to a desk in one corner and cleared off a stack of newspapers to make room.

Liz's response to the embroidered muslin contrasted with the members of the Hook and Needle Club. Rather than exclaim, Liz stared thoughtfully at the embroidery for the longest time, offering no comment. Feeling awkward in the face of her silence, Annie told the story of how and where she had found the piece, and shared the conclusions of the Hook and Needle Club. Annie even produced the cartoon map that seemed to replicate the lines of the embroidery.

Liz nodded slowly to acknowledge Annie's words but

remained silent. Finally, she craned her neck around and called toward the back room, "Hank, you're awfully quiet. You still here?"

"That I am," came a disembodied response.

"Well, I think you'll want to see this."

A thin, wiry man, short and energetic, with untamed gray curls covering most of his head, almost bounded out of the back room. Liz introduced him as Hank Page, adding, "He's helping us create a computer archive of our records. Hank, Annie is Betsy Holden's granddaughter."

"Ah," he reached out and shook Annie's hand, cupping his left hand over hers. "The Holdens were good people."

Liz turned to the embroidery. "Annie brought in this. What do you make of it?"

Turning his attention to the desk for the first time, Hank nearly jumped. He seemed to be quivering with energy, and he stepped close, patting his pockets until he located a pair of reading glasses. While Hank bent over the muslin and looked at it carefully, examining the Xs and the notations on the back, Liz explained to Annie that Hank was a retired accounting professor and amateur local historian.

"I think it's a map," Annie repeated to Hank, holding out the cartoon map.

He nodded without looking up or at what Annie had in her hands. "I do believe it is, yes … hmm … most unusual."

Finally he took off his reading glasses, folding them up and slipping them into his shirt pocket. "I can't speak to the quality of the embroidery, though it does look to be very fine. But yes, it appears to represent the local coastline. A map of sorts, as you say. The contours—well, the details look to me to be just right. We can compare it to something more authoritative, but my sense is that this is a remarkably accurate representation." He shook his head in admiration. "At this point I can only guess at its origin." Hank chuckled modestly. "My first guess is that it was made in the nineteenth century, when there was a lot of shipping traffic in this area. Perhaps it was a young woman's gift to her sailor beau or husband, or something a young wife did to keep occupied during the months her husband was away at sea ... but it definitely needs some study." He glanced questioningly at Liz, who nodded in confirmation of all that he'd said.

"I'm sure that would be a welcome project for the Historical Society, Annie," she said. "In fact," she seemed to work out the idea even as she spoke it, "if you would be willing to loan it to us, we could display it, even build a nice exhibit around it, while it is being researched." It was her turn to give her colleague a questioning look. "Now that the baskets are done."

Hank nodded vigorously. "Oh, indeed, indeed. That's a wonderful idea. Our members treasure personal links to local history, and I believe this might just be something very special for the community." He turned to Liz. "We've got that ship's log and navigation charts. And the seascapes ..."

"Yes, and this could be the centerpiece," Liz said, picking up his enthusiasm. But she stopped herself and turned back to Annie. "Though, only if you're willing, of course. Naturally, we'll give you credit for the loan of the piece. However you'd like to have it worded ..."

"Well, not just yet!" Annie said, somewhat taken aback.

"I mean, I'd love to have you display it, if you really think it justifies the attention. But, well, Grace Emory at the library did suggest I show it to someone at the Maine Folk Arts Center in West Waring—"

Liz and Hank spoke simultaneously:

"Oh yes, that could be helpful."

"I wouldn't waste my time there!"

Annie frowned in surprise at Hank's sudden vehemence, but Liz diffused the tension with a playful punch on his shoulder. "Hank doesn't often see eye to eye with the director there," she said.

Hank smiled ruefully. "It's not really that, but I suppose it won't do any harm for Gus to take a look." He looked back down at the embroidery spread on the desk and then pulled a cell phone from his pocket. "Would you mind if I took a picture of it before you go?"

Annie gestured for him to go ahead, and he began to carefully weight down the corners of the muslin with a few snow globes, a paperweight, and an old metal stapler.

As Hank worked, Liz offered to call ahead to the Folk Arts Center on Annie's behalf. "You'll find them a bit more knowledgeable than we are, I'm afraid, about decorative arts periods and trends in Maine, though we'd be happy to help you research this piece. Hank especially. He's written some wonderful tracts about our area's significance in American history. He's a careful researcher who really knows how to find a story in all the arcane minutia and records left behind."

"Now, Liz," he murmured deprecatingly as he turned the piece over to photograph the back.

"The Pages have lived in this area since, well, you tell her, Hank."

"Jacob Page was a commodore in the Navy in the War of 1812, and he settled here afterward to become a somewhat successful trader with a small fleet of ships. But he was originally from Massachusetts, so to that extent the Pages are, to use the common phrase, 'from away.' "

Liz laughed and explained to Annie the inside joke is reputed to have come from a rather contentious town meeting many years ago where a tie vote was broken by counting which side had more native Maine votes. "Back then, if you couldn't trace your local ancestry back to before the Revolution, you were a newcomer."

"There!" Hank peered at the images on the screen of his cell phone, thumbing a tiny button to cycle through them. "Newfangled technology comes in handy some days. Do you have an e-mail address? I'd be happy to send you a copy."

Before Annie was allowed to leave the Cultural Center, she was presented with a copy of each of Hank's tracts and pamphlets, which he autographed for her with an old fountain pen dipped in India ink. Annie knew, though, that her grandparents had copies of most of these booklets. Nevertheless, she was glad to have made Hank's acquaintance and glad to have the help researching the embroidery. She sensed she would be less likely to go in circles with a couple of experienced historians at work with her.

6

On Thursday Annie called the Maine Folk Arts Center in West Waring and made a Friday appointment to talk with the head curator, Gus St. Pierre.

A cold rain had blown in, so she spent most of Thursday reading, with Boots curled up on her lap. From her library books, Annie learned all about the craze for weaving in the forties. The illustrations of tablecloths with intricate overshot patterning were especially compelling. The patterns of the weave had an undulating aspect that recalled the embroidery piece, but the weavers were working a design that had regularly repeating motifs. These patterns were not intended to represent something real in the way that Annie's embroidery did.

In her mind, Annie called it *her* embroidery, but she didn't really feel that it was something she owned; she thought of it as belonging to the public, the way a Picasso, regardless of who owns it, may be seen and loved by many. Perhaps the eagerness of Liz and Hank to display it had influenced her. But as she considered this, Annie also began to better understand her own need to learn more about the piece. To own such a work carried a measure of responsibility, she thought. It may have been stitched in private, but it was meant to be looked at, admired, even studied. In fact, Annie doubted that the artist had worked in private. One thing she did know about needlecraft is that it is handed down from one generation to the next. It is taught—by grandmothers, by stitching groups. In those tight, sinuous chain stitches might reside a history of a friendship forged when two people sat down to pass on the craft.

* * * *

Friday was a beautiful spring day, if still a little chilly. As Annie stepped out onto her porch, the yard and the lilac bushes were teeming with robins, chickadees, towhees, and a couple of red-winged blackbirds. *Making up for lost time yesterday*, Annie thought, and she headed toward her Malibu.

The drive inland was lovely too. The green of spring was struggling to erupt, despite the chill weather. Soon New England's vernal explosion would be upon them.

West Waring was a small town built around a green. A simple two-story white clapboard church at one end was encased in scaffolding; apparently the steeple was being repaired. At the other end of the green was an ornate brick building with a mansard roof, pointed Gothic windows, and a round tower. It had once been a school, but now the Crossman Complex, as it was called, housed a number of offices, including the Maine Folk Arts Center. Despite boasting a block-long row of brick commercial buildings, the town exuded a sense of stillness. Annie thought of that moment in church between the ending of a prayer and the spoken "amen."

Annie found parking along the street near the church

and enjoyed a window-shopping stroll in the sunshine as she made her way to the Folk Arts Center.

A brightly colored flag announced the Center, suggesting a museum taking up all three floors of the Crossman Complex, but in reality the Folk Arts Center occupied only one side of the first floor of the building. Lawyers and real estate agents, a dentist, and a hair stylist occupied the remaining floors.

Annie opened the glass door of the Folk Arts Center and was a little surprised to find that it was really more of a gallery than a museum. The long, narrow space was light and airy. Tapestries, oil paintings, and watercolors hung on the walls, and in the center of the room was a large sculpture made of polished driftwood. Along one side was a glass display case of expensive jewelry for sale. She'd barely had time to turn around when a tall, thin man stepped up and introduced himself as August St. Pierre.

"I'm Annie Dawson, from Stony Point. My, what a lovely place!" Annie gestured toward the artwork on the wall. She hoped she didn't betray her feelings of disappointment that it was so small. "Liz Booth spoke highly of what you've done here, Mr. St. Pierre."

"Please, call me Gus." He smiled and bowed his head slightly. "Let me show you around, and then we can take a look at your … embroidery piece, is it?"

Annie nodded. Gus had wispy blond-gray hair, an early summer tan, and a graceful way of moving.

"As you enter, the pieces here are all by local artists, and they are for sale," he began, gesturing toward the works in question. "The Center takes a small commission, which is how we finance our research. Further back, the items on display are not for sale but are part of the Center's scholarly and educational mission. That large piece over the jewelry case is an Agnes Burke," he glanced at Annie to see if she responded to the name. When she did not, he continued, "Her work is mostly shown in Boston and New York, but she summers here in West Waring. We are fortunate to have some of her work to display and sell. She has been a good friend to the Center and often drops by when she's in town.

"Now, if you'll step over here," Gus motioned to the back of the room, "you'll see our special exhibit on Maine puffins as rendered by local artists."

Annie was struck by the whimsical ways the colorful birds were captured. She smiled and admitted, "I've yet to see a puffin, believe it or not."

"Oh, they are coming back from the brink of extinction, so I expect you'll see one soon enough, especially if you go sailing out of Rockport."

"That will have to wait at least for a little warmer weather, I'm afraid. I'm still getting acclimated to the weather in New England."

"Liz told me you moved here from Texas not too long ago, and that you've been cleaning out your grandmother's home." Gus ushered Annie into a workroom behind the gallery area. "And here" he said, "is where the magic happens: the research, the conservation, the analysis." The room was lined with shelves and cabinets, all crammed with artifacts. In the center of the room was a large, not very magical-looking worktable, and Annie placed her felted tote bag at one end and pulled out the muslin.

"It was suggested to me that you might help me identify this."

"Oh my!" Gus exclaimed as Annie spread the fabric out on the table. "It is indeed as lovely as Liz described. You found it, Liz said, in your grandparents' attic?"

"Yes. In a box of dishes. I don't think my grandmother ever saw it."

"Hmm ..." Gus switched on a powerful lamp on a swinging arm and positioned it over the muslin. He bent over it, examining the embroidery minutely. While he did so, Annie's eyes roamed over the curiosities that filled cubbyholes along the walls and on top of the filing cabinets. *It is a shame*, she thought, *that some of what's back here isn't out front.*

"Humph," he said, and mumbled something to himself that Annie couldn't make out. "Well, I have my hunches, but at this point they are just that."

"I'm sure your hunches are a lot more educated than mine would ever be."

"Well, I would bank on this being a piece of tourist art, of a kind that was popular from around the turn of the century up until about the 1920s." Gus spoke without looking up from the embroidery.

"Tourist art?"

"For the tourist market—objects made to be sold to tourists." He straightened up and smiled. "Oh, I don't mean that derogatorily. Or, not necessarily. Art needs its patrons, and Maine's been a tourist mecca since the Vikings first set foot here."

"What about the seal and the cormorant and the sun and moon?" Annie asked.

"Decorative embellishments. They would have increased the value." He tapped the muslin. "There are some interesting contradictions here. The intricate samplers—that is, the pieces women made for their own homes or as gifts—usually have the embroiderer's initials incorporated into the design, as you see here in the corner." Gus St. Pierre pointed to the tiny letters YSP embedded in the splash of water around the seal. "But the intricacy of the stitch work and the almost photographic quality of the representation makes me think that one person perhaps drew out the design but then had a few hired girls do the actual embroidery. So probably more than one person worked on this."

"I see. And what do you think of the Xs?" Annie asked.

"Yes." He drew the word out with a puzzled tone. "Not a part of the work as planned, I think. They may have been something the embroiderer put in to mark a space, something she, or they, would have taken out when it was finished."

"It looks complete to me," Annie protested. Then she forced herself to smile. She was grateful for his insights, but she couldn't help but feel that this erudite and charming man was holding something back.

"Tell me again how long this has been in your family?"

"Oh—oh." Annie was caught a little off guard. "No, I wouldn't say it like that. I found it in my grandmother's attic."

"That's right, excuse me. You said it was hidden in an old cookie jar. What did the jar look like?"

"Ah, boy," Annie stammered. "Not hidden. I don't think my grandmother knew it was there. It was in a box of dishes, each individually wrapped in paper. I doubt the person who had wrapped up the dishes even knew it was there. Knowing my grandmother, I think she bought the entire box of dishes at a yard sale without inspecting them carefully."

"Yard sale? Where? There wouldn't have been a sales receipt for the box, by any chance?"

"Receipt?" Exasperated, Annie laughed, and began to fold up the muslin, trying to make her actions seem as innocent as possible, but in truth, this Gus St. Pierre was starting to make her uncomfortable with his persistent questions. "Really that was just speculation on my part. I was hoping I could learn more about the piece's history from you."

"Yes. Of course. You must forgive my 'historian's curiosity.' " He bowed his head a little. "In cases like this, one must act like a detective, you see. The smallest clue could make the connection that yields the object's secrets."

Mollified, Annie chalked his behavior up to his passion as a historian.

Gus nodded and absentmindedly scratched his chin. After a moment, he said, "Do you think I might hang onto the piece for a while?" He watched her face carefully as he said this. "Perhaps show it to some colleagues," he continued, quickly adding, "I will be happy to give you a receipt for it, of course."

Annie clutched the felted tote to her ribs and explained that she had already promised to lend the embroidery piece to the Stony Point Historical Society and that they planned to exhibit it. She hadn't mentioned Hank's name, but she noticed Gus stiffen slightly at the mention of the Historical Society. He seemed about to say something, thought better of it, and instead suavely responded that he understood.

"Perhaps I'll come see it again there. If I may?"

As they walked back through the gallery, Gus pointed out to Annie the Center's small book corner. They did seem to have a decent selection packed into a small space, though as she quickly scanned the titles, Annie noticed that there were no copies of Hank Page's works. Taking up one of his own local history pamphlets, Gus presented it to Annie as a complimentary copy.

"I wrote my master's thesis on maritime commerce in Maine," he explained, tapping its cover. "Subsequently, I removed the boring parts, leaving me with this small volume." Annie thought the self-deprecation sounded a tad rehearsed, but he insistently pressed the tract into her hands until she accepted it.

She smiled and thanked him as graciously as she could, but she was strangely glad to pass through the Center's doors back into the bright sunshine of the day.

7

The wonderful Two Ewe yarn was now completely sold out at A Stitch in Time. In its place, Mary Beth had assembled a display of sock yarn, tacking to the top and sides of the cubbyholes a colorful assembly of mittens, socks, and hats that could be made with just one or two skeins. Most of the items, Annie knew, had been made by Mary Beth's customers, many under her expert guidance, and they had lent their projects just for this display. The effect was that of a stage curtain that invited shoppers in to touch and compare colors and weights, and start planning simple "weekend" projects.

"Ah, but one has to think 'fall' when knitting in the spring," Stella said, a little wistfully, and Annie turned to see her loading up a basket with an assortment of green and brown earth-toned yarns.

"What are you thinking of doing?" Annie asked. She enjoyed hearing about her friends' projects as much as she enjoyed crocheting herself.

"Fair Isle mittens, and those—what do you call them? Gloves that have no fingers?"

"Fingerless gloves," floated the voice of Mary Beth from somewhere beyond the yarn.

Annie cocked an eyebrow at Stella, and they followed the voice deeper into the store.

"Yes, yes, fingerless gloves," Stella muttered, settling into her usual seat for the Hook and Needle Club's weekly meeting.

No sooner had all the women shown off what they had been working on over the week than Kate blurted out, "Well, Annie. Tell us about the map. Have you figured out whodunit yet?"

Annie chuckled. "Well, let's see … everyone I've talked to agrees that it is indeed a map of the coast around the Stony Point area, but so far, I have gleaned just a few educated guesses about its origins. It could be 'tourist art,' or it might have been lovingly made for a husband away at sea. It could date from the late eighteen hundreds, or it could have been made in the 1920s. But in any event, I do seem to have help now. At the Historical Society, Hank Page has promised to help me look into it, as did the man who runs the Maine Folk Arts Center in West Waring."

"That would be one of the St. Pierres. August, I think," Gwendolyn mused.

"Gus, right," Annie confirmed. "Inquisitive fellow—"

"Acquisitive, I think you mean," Stella interjected. That was followed by an uncomfortable silence in the room. "Well, the St. Pierres are well known in these parts," she added defensively.

Gwendolyn noticed Annie looking a little lost at this turn in the conversation and explained, "The St. Pierres are from away—Canada, to be more specific. The family had a reputation for doing business under the table, but really, Stella, that was years ago, before young Gus's time. Gus has done us all a tremendous service by supporting local artists the way he does with the Folk Arts Center. And his sister Vivienne revived the West Waring Garden Club, and they've been sprucing up the town with their annual lilac festival and plantings."

"Besides, the St. Pierres were never as bad as their cousins," added Alice. "They suffered by their association with the Burkes."

"The Burkes were a bad lot," agreed Stella.

Annie frowned. "Gus mentioned a woman named Burke, an artist."

"Really?" Stella asked sharply. "I thought they'd all left the area."

"It's true the St. Pierres have come up in the world," Peggy said, "but in the process, they've also hurt people with their snobbishness. I don't mean to speak ill of them, but the minute a St. Pierre comes into The Cup & Saucer, the vibe suddenly turns chilly. Not that they *deign* to stick their noses in our door except once in a blue moon."

Dropping her knitting in her lap, Gwendolyn said, "I'm afraid Peggy's right, but their own family was once ostracized too. Some of what seems like snobbery may just be a form of self-protection. That's the sort of thing that can get handed down in families."

"Gwendolyn, you're too fair," Stella said, foisting her knitting over to her. "Now will you be my angel? I've dropped a stitch, and I'm having trouble seeing it. Here's a crochet hook. Can you see if you can bring it up for me?"

"Back to my embroidery piece—" Annie began, to which the women responded encouragingly. "The good news is the Historical Society wants to display it; I guess they're going to create some sort of exhibit. The hope is that when they do so, someone may come forward with new information. I delivered it to Liz Booth yesterday so she can get a display ready for it."

"Liz does a terrific job with the Historical Society exhibits," Stella said. "It's in good hands now, Annie."

"Will she have one of her openings for the exhibit?" asked Gwendolyn. "Those are always exciting events. Remember the one she did for the exhibit of old tools? It was the social event of the season."

"Oh, yes, and she had that contest to guess what some of the odder tools were," Alice said. "That was so much fun. What was that one that nobody could guess? A scrap? Something like that."

"At least there were no fights at that one," Stella said.

"Stella, that wasn't a fight!" Peggy protested. Turning to Annie, she explained, "Another year, there was a little disagreement over whose family had been the first in the area to use engines in their lobster boats."

"Well, I don't know about an opening," Annie said. "She didn't say anything about that. But Hank Page gave me a JPEG of the picture he took so I can—"

"A what?" Stella asked.

"An electronic copy of a picture he took with his cell phone. It's a pretty good picture. I downloaded it onto my computer to use as my desktop image, and I e-mailed it to my daughter to show her what kind of trouble I've been getting into."

To Annie's surprise, the idea of using the picture as a desktop image was popular among her fellow stitchers, who all asked for a copy—all but Stella, who guffawed and insisted that Annie was now speaking some foreign language.

Kate jumped up when she saw a customer approaching the cash register and returned with the news that someone had managed to find one last Two Ewe skein tucked in among the bulky yarns and had just bought it.

"Speaking of yarns," Mary Beth segued somewhat pointedly, "where are we with the projects for the Coynes?"

"Well, Stella and I met over the weekend and put the finishing touches on the mitered-corner afghan," Gwendolyn volunteered.

"And I finished the curtains with some piping that I think adds some interest," Peggy said, pulling out some muted sand-colored fabric that was bordered with the same deep red Stella had used in some of her mitered squares.

"Lovely," Mary Beth exclaimed. "Peggy, you are so clever with fabric." Peggy was an avid quilter, often warning those who expressed interest in the craft of its addictiveness.

When the group had the projects, including the cookie jar, gathered together on a table, it was obvious that their collection would be too much for one box. As the women went about refolding and arranging the items into two boxes, Mary Beth pulled Annie aside.

"I'm going to let Kate handle the store for a while and go right on over. Why don't you join me? Laura Coyne is expecting us."

Annie was a little taken aback by the sudden suggestion, but the fact was, she'd been wanting to meet the Coynes' daughter ever since she saw her in the library.

"I'd be happy to help. Oh—" Annie hesitated, suddenly

feeling insecure when she saw Peggy gently nestle the cookie jar among some knitted throw pillows. "Do you really think the cookie jar is appropriate right now? I mean, it has a chip in the back—"

"Believe me," Mary Beth assured her, "Laura will love it. She had quite a collection of old dishes, and she loved the heavy diner mugs and creamers. Now, all of it is gone." Mary Beth snapped her fingers. "Just like that."

"You know, Annie," Alice piped in, "I bet she would love to have some of the other items you found in that box. Not that I mean to be giving away your possessions." Alice laughed at herself. "It's just that they are all of a similar style as the cookie jar, and now that they are settled someplace, presumably they will need more housewares."

"I would love to see someone who enjoys old dishes take them. I think my grandmother would too. I was just thinking. When we saw the Coyne girl in the library, I believe she was holding an Agatha Christie novel. If she likes mysteries, I've got a few good ones I can include."

"Great!" Mary Beth bellowed, startling a customer near the front of the store, who left hurriedly without buying anything. "We'll just drop by your place on the way over and pick them up."

That settled, the other women slowly began to leave. Gwendolyn stopped by the sock-yarn display and picked out a self-striping variegated yarn and a hat pattern. At the cash register she commented to Kate that pompoms weren't exactly her forte.

"Don't worry. I'll make them for you when you are ready to put on the finishing touches," Kate assured her.

* * * *

In her SUV, Mary Beth followed Annie home and supervised Annie's repacking of the dishes in a bigger box. She helped select a handful of paperbacks, tossing aside any that were deemed too dark or "infernal" for a young mind who'd just experienced a tragedy. Then the two women set out together in Mary Beth's car for the Coynes' new apartment.

Mary Beth took a small detour to her own house as well. Annie waited in the car while she ran in, and then as they resumed the trip, Mary Beth pulled to the curb across and just down the street from the blackened remains of the Coynes' home. She sat and stared at it for a moment.

"I didn't really know David Coyne before the fire, only Laura and Megan mostly, but I've come to have a lot of respect for that man, and what they are saying about him just breaks my heart."

"From what I heard last week, it sounds like people are resisting the uglier speculations," Annie said. She knew Mary Beth held strong opinions, and she didn't want to say anything that would upset her the way Stella had earlier at the stitching group. "The truth will come out eventually."

"That's right," Mary Beth sighed. Her hands were poised to start driving again, but her thoughts seemed to be far away. "What I haven't said to anyone, Annie, is that I have seen David poking around what's left of the house. Both by himself and with the insurance adjuster. Annie, he always looks so defeated. I think he's just tormenting himself. There's obviously nothing to be found here."

But as Mary Beth spoke, another car, an old and battered black van with Massachusetts plates, pulled to a stop in front of the Coynes' home, facing the opposite direction. A short man with sunglasses, a black goatee, and tattoos on his bare arms got out, stretched his back as he looked around, and then sauntered over to the remains of the house. Though the spring sun was warm, Annie thought it still too chilly for the man's T-shirt.

"Who's that?" she asked.

"Don't know." The two women watched the stranger squat down on his haunches and survey the footprint of the house. "I'm going to find out, though," Mary Beth said, unlatching her seatbelt.

"Mary Beth!" Annie tried to protest, but as her friend was already charging across the street, Annie felt that all she could do was follow her.

At the sound of the car door shutting, the goateed man stood up and turned his head. When he realized that Mary Beth was headed in his direction, he quickly stepped to the van and jerked open the door.

"Excuse me, young man," Mary Beth bellowed as the door slammed and the van whined to a start. "Are you from around here?"

But the van roared off with a squeal of its tires. Annie saw the man bent low over the steering wheel, looking unswervingly ahead. After it rounded the corner at the end of the block, Annie wondered fleetingly if she should have tried to make note of the license plate number.

"Well." Mary Beth stood in the middle of the street with her arms akimbo. "I don't like that!"

Back in the car, Mary Beth explained that Stony Point's police chief himself had visited the shop to ask if she'd noticed anyone poking around the fire. "I almost threw him out of the shop. I thought he was looking for evidence against David, and of course, I have seen him there. It's only a natural human reaction to want to revisit a tragedy, to try to understand it somehow. But this fellow here is another matter."

"Chief Edwards, I'm guessing, didn't share the nature of his inquiry with you?" Annie probed.

"No. If he had, I might not have been so testy with him." Mary Beth started the engine and pulled away from the curb. "I guess a visit to the police station this afternoon is in order, and perhaps an apology."

* * * *

Annie was shocked at the dreariness of the Coynes' temporary apartment in a complex pretentiously named the Youngstown Arms. It was on the opposite side of town from their home, so she imagined the kids didn't get to play with their usual friends, nor did the complex look particularly kid-friendly, evidenced by a swing set sporting a single chain and a broken, dangling seat. Beyond the unpaved parking lot, barren except for an old car with a flat tire, two vinyl-sided buildings were crowded by hemlock trees, casting them in a gloomy shadow.

Laura Coyne was home and expecting Mary Beth and Annie. What Laura Coyne hadn't expected were the two boxes Mary Beth and Annie presented.

"Oh, oh, I don't know what to say!" she cried, covering her mouth with her hands. Her eyes started to tear up, but at that moment the teakettle whistled, and she disappeared into the kitchen to compose herself.

While Laura made tea in the kitchen, Mary Beth went about setting out the throw pillows and coasters. Then she hollered back to the kitchen, "I'm just going to take down these sheets you have in the front windows and hang up these curtains."

Laura returned from the kitchen carrying a tray of mugs of hot water, an assortment of tea bags, and paper napkins. She and Annie exchanged looks of recognition. Mary Beth was a powerhouse.

"I can't believe you went to all that trouble for us, Mary Beth, but my, it makes a difference, doesn't it?"

"It was no trouble, dear. You know, just about all of us have had some sort of upheaval in our lives, and we got through it with a lot of leaning on friends. Friends are one of the gifts the universe gives you." Mary Beth had one end of a curtain rod in her lap, and she was threading the curtain loops onto it.

"Mary Beth, I never knew you were so mystical," Laura said, laughing a little, if partly at herself for being so emotional.

"Well, that bit of wisdom just came to me on the spot," Mary Beth said, setting aside the rod and curtain, and stirring a little sugar into her tea. "My point is, we all want to help you in whatever way you need us, and someday, someone you know, or know of, will be in a bad way, and you'll be there to help them."

"Well, Mary Beth, I hope you'll come to us when you need a friend's support."

"Count me in that, too, Mary Beth," Annie added.

"Done!" And the three women tapped their mugs together.

The three sat around a low coffee table in desperate need of refinishing. Annie and Mary Beth sat on a soiled love seat, while Laura settled in a wing chair whose brown fabric was so dark no dirt would have shown. Laura's long brown hair was pulled back in an austere ponytail, accentuating her slender neck and the fine features of her face. She was doll-like in her graceful movements, and though a little emotional at the moment, Annie sensed in her a core of strength and purpose.

After a sip of tea, Mary Beth picked up the rod and again resumed threading the curtain onto it, allowing the far end to rest in Annie's lap.

"I do believe, though, that our environment has a tremendous effect on how we go about our daily lives," continued Mary Beth. "We need sunlight and cheer and comfort, we do." Though with the windows now completely uncovered, the sunlight falling against the unadorned wall struck Annie as rather harsh. *Even such a boon as light,* she thought, *sometimes needs the moderating influence of human ingenuity.*

Mary Beth stood to carry the rod and curtain to the window. As she did so, they heard the rumble and plaintive moan of a large vehicle braking to a stop in the parking lot. Laura said, "That will be the school bus." Mary Beth, who had started to lift the rod to the brackets, lowered it again with a smile of delight and looked down into the lot to watch the arrival. She gazed out for several moments, and Annie saw a frown of dismay suddenly darken her features. Mary Beth drew a breath as if to speak, but before she did so, the chaotic clumping and banging and chatter of Megan and Martin announced their progress up the stairs and into the living room.

"Mary Beth!" they shouted at once, running over and accepting a hug. For a moment, they were enfolded by the still unhung curtain.

Martin had been half out of his shoes when he entered the living room, and turning from Mary Beth, he sloughed them off and tossed them to the corner. Laura coughed, reminding the children that they had company. Martin and Megan both stood still and shook Annie's hand when Laura introduced them; then Martin giggled and tromped sock-footed into the kitchen in search of a snack. Megan sat ladylike on the edge of a wooden chair. She seemed shy in Annie's presence and uncomfortable making conversation, but she was grown up enough to sit quietly and respectfully with the older women.

"I've heard that you are becoming a fine knitter," Annie said to Megan, hoping to draw her out of her shell, but the girl blushed deeply and bowed her head. *Why do young girls go underground when they hit twelve?* Annie wondered, recalling how she had suddenly become intensely self-conscious and self-critical during her own painful adolescence.

"She sure is!" Mary Beth had finally hung the curtain, and after admiring the sight for a moment (and taking another quick look out the window), she resumed her seat.

"I even have one of her scarves on display at the store. It's in green heather wool with a checkerboard pattern."

"Oh, yes, I saw that," Annie said. She exchanged a smile with Megan.

"Her daddy gave her a hard ribbing about that, Mary Beth," Laura said. "He thought he'd get to wear it before summer rolled in."

"Well, now he'll have it for next winter," Mary Beth reported. "That's the thing about New England. Winter comes 'round every year, whether you want it to or not."

"He used to wear a red one that I made for him," Megan clarified, "but it burned. I also want to make him some fingerless gloves to wear when he's at work. The garage gets real cold. Even in the summer, it's cold."

"That sounds like a good project for using up leftover yarn," Annie added.

"Oh, I almost forgot this," Mary Beth said reaching for another box. "Look what we found … and thought you might like." She pulled out the clown cookie jar and delicately set his hat in place.

Laura reached for the cookie jar and gave it a close inspection. "Mary Beth, I can't take this from you."

"Of course you can. It's from Annie."

"I mean, it's a collector's item. See?" Laura set the hat on the table and turned over the bottom of the jar to show Mary Beth and Annie the maker's mark on the bottom. She set it down and covered her mouth again with her hand, starting to cry a little. Megan edged over to put her arm around her mother. "You see," Laura said, "I—I had a book just on this type of pottery."

Mary Beth reached over and placed a soothing hand on Laura's knee. "What this fella needs is someone who appreciates him, and we all felt that would be you and Megan and Martin and David. He's yours."

"I'd really be very pleased if you'd take the cookie jar," Annie added. To give Laura a chance to compose herself, she told again the story of finding it.

Laura took a calming sip of tea. "Oh, me." She smiled a little and dabbed her eyes with a napkin. "You'll have to forgive me. I've been up and down since the fire. Crying one moment, laughing hysterically the next."

"Daddy won't let her talk about it," Megan ventured. "We're not allowed to use the word fire when he's around."

"He's just trying to keep us sane," Laura said. "speak of the devil," she added, hearing a car door slam.

There was a hush in the room while they waited for David to enter, but the wait seemed to stretch a little longer than it should for him to cross the parking lot and climb the stairs.

Mary Beth had taken up another rod and was busily threading another curtain. Finally, she looked up at Laura and said, "Will you help with this?"

With a puzzled look on her face, Laura stepped over to the uncurtained window, which also looked onto the parking lot. Her puzzlement changed to something harder and darker as she looked out, but she didn't say anything. Since both Mary Beth and Laura had now seen something through the window that they clearly didn't like, Annie was intensely curious. Trying to behave as casual as possible, she stood and drifted over to the window herself. "I always like curtains for windows," she said in an effort to further justify her action, but she was barely able to stifle a gasp when she looked out.

Two men were holding an animated discussion in the parking lot. One she took to be David Coyne; he looked vaguely familiar, as if she'd seen him around town. The other was the tattooed and goateed driver of the van with Massachusetts plates.

She turned quickly to find that Mary Beth was watching her intently, but as soon as she moved, Mary Beth jumped up with the second rod and curtain in hand and approached the second window.

"Here we go, then," she said brightly, hanging the rod on its brackets. "Now they match again." Annie took her cue and said nothing about the strange, goateed man.

Soon enough they heard David's heavy steps climbing the stairs. He paused at the door, took a breath, and exhaled heavily. "Mary Beth," he said with exaggerated heartiness. "Always good to see you!" He bent over and kissed Laura on the head, and feigned injury when Martin, rushing in from the kitchen, bulldozed into him.

"Honey, this is Annie Dawson, a friend of Mary Beth's from the Hook and Needle Club," Laura said. David sat down in the spot where Megan had just been.

"And look what the ladies made for us, Dad," Megan burst in excitedly.

"Yup. Very nice." David was laconic by nature, but he listened with interest and his eyes smiled gently as Megan and Laura showed off the projects from the Hook and Needle Club. He was tall and big, with muscular hands that still bore traces of black oil. "And who's this fellow?" David started to reach for the clown, but Megan and Laura both lurched, and Laura edged it out of his grasp.

He held up his hands to show their guests. "Don't know why the women folk around here are afraid of a little grease."

"Well, my dears," Mary Beth said setting down her tea mug. "Time is moving on, and I need to head back to the store and relieve Kate."

Annie stood up and was surprised when Laura stood up with her and gave her a hug.

"You guys—" Laura said, starting to cry a little again.

"Mary Beth, Annie." David shook their hands. "Thank you for everything." David gestured with his hands at the room and his wife, who was still crying a little as Mary Beth and Annie made their way out the door.

* * * *

"Well," Mary Beth said as soon as her SUV was back on the road, "I think we did a good turn for the Coynes today, but I don't know what to think of that man with the tattoos. You saw him, too, didn't you? Did you see him talking to David?"

"I did, but it's no use jumping to conclusions. They will most certainly be wrong," Annie warned her, but it was clear from her expression that Mary Beth's mind was running over all possibilities.

"You're right. I know you're right, but I can't help thinking that that man was harassing David." Mary Beth's hands were gripping the steering wheel so tightly that her knuckles were turning white.

"Mary Beth—"

"No, you're right. I'm letting myself get ahead of the facts." She slowed to stop at an intersection in the road and stretched her fingers for a minute. Annie craned her neck to scan the road ahead and the crossroad as far as she could see. Despite her admonition to Mary Beth, she half expected to see the battered black van idling off the side of the road, waiting for Mary Beth's SUV to pass by.

"Look!" Mary Beth pointed up ahead at a ramshackle farm stand with a hand-lettered sign out front. "Strawberries! Annie, this will only take a minute. Do you mind?"

Annie followed Mary Beth into the old farm stand. Pints of strawberries lined the rear wall behind a table holding varieties of salad greens and a healthy crop of asparagus. Annie couldn't resist a quart of berries and even bought some to freeze for later on. But Mary Beth had drifted off to the attached greenhouse to look over flats of petunias and pansies. Putting her purchase in the car first, Annie intended to join Mary Beth, but she espied a forgotten old graveyard through the new spring foliage and the tug of curiosity propelled her forward.

The small cemetery was overgrown and hemmed in by a dilapidated wrought-iron fence. Lettering above the gate announced the Youngstown Cemetery.

She stepped over the brambles, and giving the gate a shove to push it over the unmown grass, stepped inside the little enclosure, pulling her legs up and over the thick, tall grass as she did. The slender white marble markers bore little in the way of adornment—no carved doves or evergreens, just thin white marble stones and short inscriptions, many of which were in French. She noticed that a number of markers shared the same year of death, suggesting that epidemics of some sort had come through at different points in this small enclave's history.

She kept an eye out for women's names with the initials YSP, but found none, not even among the child graves, of which, she noted, there were many.

The wind suddenly died, and Annie found herself in an eerie stillness. She kept marching through the stones, shivering a little in the damp, cool air, until she could take the oppressive atmosphere no more and returned to the car.

Mary Beth soon appeared in the door of the greenhouse, followed by a young boy pulling a wagon loaded with flower plants. Mary Beth turned and tipped the youngster a dollar, and Annie helped her load the plants into the back of her SUV.

"Look back there," Annie said to Mary Beth as she was hustling back into the car. "An old cemetery."

Mary Beth cocked her head and nodded. "That's what's left of Youngstown."

"Oh? So there really was a Youngstown at some point. I thought it was just a name a developer came up with."

"There really was such a place, till it was flattened by a hurricane in the thirties. It's odd how fortune can change so quickly. You think misfortune will never happen to you, and then poof!" Mary Beth started the car, echoing "poof" one more time before pulling back out onto the road.

* * * *

Armed with two quarts of strawberries that needed attending to, Annie was nevertheless relieved to be back home after a long day. The visit with Laura Coyne had been emotionally draining, and she wanted nothing more than to sit on the porch with a glass of iced tea and look out over the ocean in silence.

That was not to be. First, Boots met her at the kitchen door with a howl. She had not appreciated being home alone all day and was ready for some lap time with Annie. Then, much to Boots's and Annie's dismay, their peaceful afternoon was interrupted by a visit from Mike Malone, owner of the hardware store and publisher of The Point, who was doing a write-up on the Historical Society's upcoming exhibit.

"Hank Page thinks you've got quite a find," he said, casually resting a foot on the front step. "I gather it's of particular interest to the old-timers of Stony Point."

"Well, I don't know about that," Annie said laughing. "But it's certainly a beautiful piece. The stitch work is amazing. It appears to be a rendition of the coastline of this part of Maine, and the care and detail the maker put into this 'map' is just astounding."

Mike asked her to tell again the story of finding the embroidery, and he wrote furiously on his notepad as she spoke.

"And you don't think Mrs. Holden knew the map was in the cookie jar?" he asked.

"Well, that's just a guess on my part, of course, but no, I don't. I think if she'd known it was there, she'd have done something with it. Perhaps the Historical Society could have had their exhibit a long time ago." She smiled at the reporter, though she wondered just what her grandmother would have done with the embroidery piece if she'd been the one to pull it from the cookie jar.

Mike Malone frowned and tapped his pen on his skinny reporter's notebook for a few moments; then he looked up and winked. "This should do it, Annie, and thank you for your time. Look for it on Thursday. Good day."

8

Light poured out into the warm spring evening from the windows and doors of the Cultural Center as the residents of Stony Point crowded into the Historical Society's exhibit space for the opening of "Artifacts." The hum of conversation and laughter spilled out into the street as Annie and Alice approached.

"My word," said Annie in a subdued tone.

"I told you," said Alice. "Liz throws a great party. She hasn't had one in a couple of years, but these opening receptions are always the talk of the town." She dropped her voice and drawled, "It's the start to the social season, dahling. Absolutely tout le monde will be there."

And that seemed to be the case. Annie quickly spotted most of her friends from the Hook and Needle Club, but before she could approach them, Liz Booth had swept up beside her. "Our heroine! Annie, I can't thank you enough for lending us the embroidery. It's generated so much interest, and it inspired Hank to outdo himself in assembling this exhibit. It was just the catalyst we needed."

Liz took her by the elbow and conducted her on a tour of the exhibit. Around the perimeter of the room was an eclectic assembly of quilts, toboggans, iron cookware, woodsman's tools, handmade dolls, weather vanes, and other items, each one with some connection to local history, and most with a direct connection to people living in Stony Point, which made the exhibit all the more interesting.

"Have you heard about the King recorders?" Liz asked, and she drew Annie to a display case filled with the wooden musical instruments in a variety of sizes. "This was a local family," Liz continued, "and for years their recorders were the best in the country. All handmade by three generations of the family. They were shipped all over the world." Annie dutifully examined the instruments, along with a photo from the 1930s of an all-recorder marching band.

Though the Kings were apparently now gone, and their company sold, Annie was pleased to find a number of donor names that she recognized: Besham, Page, Coyne, Pushee. "Yes," Liz said when Annie remarked on the familiar names, "many families have deep roots in this community, and they've been generous in giving or lending us items."

One section of wall was devoted to Franco-American recipes from the cookbook of Marie Bishop for dishes such as creton (pork pâté), tourtiere (pork pie), and beignes (doughnuts). This display made Annie's mouth water, and she turned to the sadly more mundane crudités, celery sticks, and broccoli florets arranged around a bowl of dip.

Garnering the most interest, though, was a glass display case that showcased Annie's map, along with some of Hank's extensive notes. The crowd was thickest here, and Annie could hear many people discussing it.

"Alice, I don't get it," she said in her friend's ear. "Everything in this exhibit is so fascinating, not just the map."

"I know, but you have to understand that many of these artifacts have been displayed before, or they're things people just grew up with," Alice explained. "The map is truly new, so it's a sensation."

Just then a small bell sounded, drawing the guests' attention and silencing the chatter. Stella Brickson, as the driving force for getting the Cultural Center opened, now had the honor of presiding at events like this. And she did it well: She had a commanding, regal presence, and when she spoke, Annie could almost imagine she was descended from royalty. Stella wore a soft pink-and-gray dress with a matching coat and large gray pearl beads and earrings that seemed to be backlit by her beautifully coiffed gray hair.

Stella greeted the crowd and praised Liz Booth and Hank Page for their efforts in organizing the exhibit. She then told the story of how Annie's map had been found. Annie gave a rueful smile and raised her plastic cup of white wine to acknowledge the crowd's applause. Stella concluded by turning over the podium (such as it was) to Hank, the curator of the featured exhibit.

Hank had the air of a scholar in thrall to his subject, as he stepped to the front of the crowd and began to speak. His eyes were intense, and his hair was as wild as ever. He'd dressed up for the event in an old sport coat with frayed leather elbow patches over a plaid shirt and tie, jeans, and shoes badly in need of resoling. To Annie he was the very embodiment of New England frugality.

As frumpish as he looked, though, he had a mesmerizing command of the audience as he peppered his speech with understated Yankee humor and dazzled everyone with an array of historical tidbits pertaining to the area. When he turned his attention to the centerpiece of the exhibit, though, he became a little more vague, his flow of words interrupted by small stammers. He talked about maps generally as indicators of how people viewed the world, and he pointed to the icons in the corner of the map as examples of coastal Maine industry: fishing and tourism. Hank said that after some consultation by phone with a Boston curator of historical textiles, he felt certain that this piece was created to be sold; close examination of the stitch work revealed that at least two and possibly three hands had worked on the map, which "contraindicated" his first assumption that it was a piece created by a young woman as a sampler or a memento of home to be sent off with a sailor beau. He started to talk about the numbered notations on the back and the letters YSP that were embedded in the design, but he didn't say much except that possibilities were still being explored.

Hank did mention that his curator friend would be visiting soon to look at the thread count of the muslin fabric, the material of the embroidery threads, and other such clues that would give a clearer picture of the age of the piece and perhaps its purpose.

The audience clapped politely, and Hank stepped back into the crowd, shaking hands with a few people. Annie herself was besieged with people asking her all sorts of questions. At one point she caught a fleeting expression of alarm cross Hank's face as he looked up—but in a second it was gone as another person pressed forward to shake his hand or to share some anecdote about Maine history.

In time, Hank made his way over to Annie, bearing a satisfied expression on his face.

"Ah. The turnout tonight does us proud, I think," he exclaimed.

"More than you had expected, I take it," Annie said.

"Well, yes, but I shouldn't be surprised. History has a lot to teach us, Annie, about ourselves. Our past clues us to what lies ahead, if you take the time to study the past, but it's things like the embroidery piece that remind us that we have a shared past and a kinship among neighbors. Ah, me ..." Hank patted his chest, which Annie thought might be a tad thrust out.

"Ah, me ..." he said again and then he smiled as an attendee stopped to shake his hand. "Between you and me," he leaned over to speak to Annie from the side of his mouth, "the piece does dovetail in an interesting way with some research I've been doing. I'm hoping to get an article out of it in the long run. It was awkward trying to keep from alluding to the new direction of my research before I have my facts checked and rechecked."

Annie looked at him sharply with raised eyebrows, to which Hank replied, "Well, why don't you drop by tomorrow afternoon so I can clue you in?"

"Yes—I think that is in order now," she said chuckling, just as another attendee swept in to buttonhole Hank with more historical minutia.

Annie turned around and scanned the room. There were so many people inside that it was hard to see, and it was getting very warm. She had started to edge her way to the door when Gus St. Pierre sidled up alongside her. With his dark blue suit of rich material and his red bow tie and pocket handkerchief, Gus was stylish elegance to Hank's threadbare academic.

Gus smiled warmly and said, "I must congratulate you on the exhibit. The other items create a cozy context for it, I think." His voice wrapped lovingly around the word it, as if the map were really the only object in the room worth speaking of. He made it sound as if the two of them shared some special appreciation of its value, not open to the philistines who surrounded them.

"Thank you," said Annie. "There are so many fascinating things here. I'm hardly the only one to donate something; though, of course, I'm happy to help."

She saw his eyes narrow. "Donate?" He said sharply and then paused. "Do you mean you've given the map to the Historical Society?"

"Sorry, I guess I should have said 'loan.' "

Gus seemed to relax slightly. "Of course. But it is the map, you know, that's brought everyone out." He smiled that conspiratorial smile again. "That's the thing everyone's eager to see." When she didn't respond, he continued, "I'm still researching it, you know. I promised to help, and I'm keeping my word. Alas, I've not yet found anything tangible. But I still have hopes."

"Thank you, Mr. St. Pierre."

"Please, please," he chided, "call me Gus." But when Annie smiled and sipped her drink without responding, he seemed at a loss for how to continue. Finally, he said, "Well, congratulations again, Annie." And with a last ingratiating smile, he turned away.

As Annie pondered this encounter, Alice returned to her side and began to guide her about the room, introducing her to some of the residents of Stony Point she did not yet know. As she circulated and conversed, Annie noticed that Hank had held court pretty much continuously by the display case with the map, showing it off to each new person who came up to have a look. Taking a brief break from socializing, she watched from a corner with interest as Gus St. Pierre stepped up to the display case.

Sensing a presence, Hank turned from another conversation. His beaming expression turned frosty in an instant. The two stood rigid with mutual dislike, and for a moment, Annie feared there might be a scene. But then they nodded stiffly to each other, and Gus bent over the case. Hank scowled for a moment at the back of his neck, but then turned and moved off to another part of the room.

As Gus leaned over the case, his nose almost touched the glass. Annie could see him methodically examining every inch of the embroidery, occasionally shifting his stance to better view a new section of the piece. This examination lasted so long that he began to monopolize access to the display case. Annie watched several people turn away after waiting for a turn. Off to one side, Liz Booth was now the one doing the scowling, and Annie wondered if Liz was going to ask Gus to step aside and give someone else a chance. Just as Liz seemed ready to speak up, however, Gus straightened abruptly and strode from the room without a glance to the right or left. Annie found herself releasing a pent-up breath.

Annie barely had time to register Gus's odd fascination with the embroidered map when Gwendolyn Palmer and her husband John breezily stepped up on either side of her and a flash exploded in her eyes. It was just a photographer for

The Point taking some candid shots of the event. As president of the Stony Point Savings Bank, which had a role in underwriting many of the Historical Society's exhibits, John Palmer made a regular appearance in the local paper and in some of the regional papers as well.

"What an extraordinary find, Annie," John said. "You're the person of the moment tonight."

"Well," Annie said, still trying to blink away the stars in her eyes, "it's just that, a find. I hadn't much luck in researching it. That's all Hank's doing."

"And Hank knows the right people doing research in other museums—I can't wait to hear what the textile conservator will have to say about this piece. Funny all the little details that say so much about something," Gwendolyn added.

The Palmers drifted off toward the door, followed by the receding sound of the camera clicking away.

* * * *

The next morning, a Saturday, Annie was surprised to find how slow she was to get moving. The exhibit opening hadn't been especially taxing, she chided herself, though perhaps the excitement had drained her more than she realized. And the fact was, she was more likely to spend evenings at home reading or crocheting than she was to spend them out. Still, she was dismayed to discover what she considered a lack of stamina.

She had settled down with her coffee and newspaper, with Boots trying to hint that a second breakfast for her would be a fine idea, when Alice knocked at the door and walked in without waiting for an answer.

"Have you heard what happened?" she asked, her eyes flashing and her cheeks flushed.

Annie looked up slowly and blinked. "This is Stony Point. I thought the whole idea was that nothing happens."

But the excitement of the news, whatever it was, carried Alice right past her friend's disappointingly uninterested response. "Not this time. This time something definitely happened."

"Well in that case, you'd better have some coffee." She waved vaguely in the direction of the pot.

Alice had just fixed her cup and settled down to share the news when there was another knock on the door. Casting Alice a questioning glance, Annie got up to answer it and was surprised indeed to find the Stony Point chief of police standing on her doorstep. Before he could speak, Annie turned toward Alice and said, "Well. I guess something really did happen."

Chief Edwards's face registered momentary confusion at this remark, but Annie quickly turned back to him and invited him in. He nodded to Alice, and Annie asked if she could get him a cup of coffee, which he accepted. "Is this about the break-in?" Alice asked.

"Attempted break-in," the chief corrected, but then he waited while Annie fixed him his coffee.

When they were all settled again, Annie said, "Break-in?"

Rather than respond directly, the chief said, "Ms. Dawson, I'm hoping you'll be willing to help me in an investigation." When she nodded, he continued, "Yes, there was an attempted break-in last night—at the Cultural Center."

"The Cultural Center!" Annie exclaimed. "But we were there last night. For the opening of the Historical Society exhibit."

Chief Edwards nodded. "Yes, ma'am. This was after that. Sometime after midnight. The reception ended about eleven, from what I'm told. But after it was over, Liz Booth and Hank Page locked up the building together. Mr. Page saw Ms. Booth to her car; then he started on home himself. He'd driven halfway home before realizing that he'd left his notes behind, so he decided to go back for them. As he crossed Main to park around behind the Cultural Center, he scared off someone who was trying to break in. He saw someone running away from the back of the building, and when he went 'round, he found that a window had been broken and forced open. So he called us."

"My word," said Annie. "Was anything stolen?"

"No, it looks like Mr. Page came by just as they were getting the window open, so they never got inside. We've had both Mr. Page and Ms. Booth looking things over to see if anything is missing, and they say nothing is."

"But, Chief, if this happened after the reception was over, I don't see how I can help you. I was home and in bed by midnight."

"Yes, ma'am, but Mr. Page feels—quite strongly feels—that what the thief was after was your ... well, he says it's a map of some sort."

"Why on earth would he think that?"

"Well, as he says, it's the only thing that's different. A lot of the stuff that's in that Historical Society is there all the time, and the other stuff that's in the exhibit is all stuff that they've had before. And no one's ever tried to mess with it. Your map is the only thing that's new, or not new new, I guess, but new to that location. That would explain why someone tried to break in last night when nobody's ever tried to do so before."

"But they've had it down there for a few days now," Annie protested, "getting ready for the exhibit."

Chief Edwards nodded. "Yes, but that's not been generally known. It wasn't until the story in the paper on Thursday and then the reception last night that a lot of people really became aware of the map's existence or knew what it looked like or where exactly to find it."

Annie glanced at Alice, who shrugged. "Of course, I'll be happy to help however I can, Chief, but I must say this sounds a little far-fetched to me."

He gave a crooked smile. "I won't deny that, though it does have a certain logic to it. But the fact is, I don't have many leads so far, so I've got to take what I can get." He paused and then continued. "I'd appreciate it if you could tell me everything you can about this map, and especially, who might be interested in possessing it." He pulled out a small notebook and set it carefully on the table next to his coffee cup.

"Just Hank," Annie said immediately, with a laugh, "or maybe Gus St. Pierre." But her laughter quickly died when she saw the serious look on the chief's face.

"St. Pierre?" he said, jotting in his notebook.

"Well, I don't want to cast suspicion on either man unnecessarily," Annie said hurriedly. "I only mean that both Gus and Hank wanted to have exclusive access to the embroidery piece to study it. Neither man strikes me as the type to steal."

The chief cocked an eyebrow at her. "I thought this was a map we were talking about?"

"It is!" Annie said, suddenly nervous, as if she'd been caught in a fib.

"It's an embroidered map," added Alice. "It shows the local coastline. It's quite beautiful."

"I have a picture of it that Hank took," said Annie, half rising. "It's on my computer. Would you like to see it?"

"Perhaps later," the chief replied. "If you could just tell me about it for now."

Annie took a sip of coffee, taking a moment to collect her thoughts. "Perhaps I should go back to how I found it in the first place." So once again she told the story of cleaning out her grandmother's attic, coming across the old clown cookie jar, and finding the embroidered map stuffed down inside. "Though I didn't realize it was a map," she said. "My friend Kate figured that out."

She described her library researches and her consultations with Liz and Hank, and with Gus St. Pierre, though she avoided saying anything about how uncomfortable Gus had made her feel. She concluded with an account of the opening the night before and of the tension she'd sensed between the two rival historians. Alice threw in some observations about the opening as well.

As Chief Edwards listened, he made only a few further notes. Mostly, he folded his hands under his arms and looked up at the ceiling, as if he were watching a movie of the story Annie was telling. When she stopped talking, he continued to stare at the ceiling for a long moment.

"The thing is," he said finally, "the summer folk are starting to arrive."

Annie and Alice exchanged questioning glances at this non sequitur. Seeing their expressions, he smiled apologetically. "What I mean is, a lot of folks are coming up weekends already, bringing their kids, who are antsy from being cooped up all winter. Sometimes the combination of warm weather and new surroundings gets them in the mood to make a little mischief. It could just be a case of vandalism, is what I'm saying. It's not unheard of this time of year, and the reception last night may have piqued somebody's interest."

He paused for thought for another moment; then he sighed and slapped his knees. "Maybe your embroidered map has got something to do with this, and maybe not. But there's no need to make things more complicated than necessary, and I don't want to worry you with speculation. Either way, the thing to do is to get my guys out there making some extra rounds in the cruiser." He stood. "I wouldn't worry about your embroidery," he said. "I'm sure it's safe. But I appreciate your time telling me about it, Ms. Dawson." He drained his cup and held it up, adding, "And I appreciate the coffee too."

And with that, Chief Edwards donned his hat and left.

"I don't know, Annie," Alice said as they watched the chief depart. "I think he's overstating the amount of vandalism the summer people bring to Stony Point."

"But not, I'm afraid, the restless energy of a teenager, and that I can tell you from experience."

"Or the restless energy of a good rumor," Alice added. "Perhaps it's best we don't say anything more about his visit if we can help it."

"I agree with you there," Annie said. "It's a nice day. How 'bout a walk on the beach?"

They jumped into Alice's Mustang and drove down Ocean Drive to the little sandy beach. With the tide just slipping out, the waves provided a gentle rumble behind the two women's conversation. The sun had burned off the morning chill but had not yet brought the full height of the day's heat. The air felt fresh and warm, and for a time, the two friends just enjoyed the fine weather. After a while, however, Annie grew thoughtful.

"Alice, what do you remember about that day the Pointer Sisters kayaked out to Caleb's Cove?"

Alice had been gazing out at the sparkling water with her hand shading her eyes. Now she glanced curiously at her friend. "All of it. Why?"

"No reason. It's just that as I was thinking back on it, I remembered hearing a radio when we were there."

"A radio? We were the only people around, as I recall."

"Yes, we were. And yet, I remember hearing—faintly—a radio playing top hits, or something like that. It was disturbing in a way, though at the time I thought so because I wanted to pretend that we were castaways from another century."

Alice smiled. "No. I don't remember the radio, but frankly, I only had eyes and ears for our instructor."

The two women paused to watch a seagull scan the rocks, looking for lunch. It was close enough that its haunting cry carried over the sound of the waves.

Annie brought her attention back to that day on the beach. "Something's made me think of that day again, and how odd it was to hear the radio just then. It's like it signaled something, but I don't know what. It just seems that it was out of place."

"Like a ghost? Or like the real world was closer than you had thought?" Alice probed.

"Oh, the latter, definitely … I mean, of course I don't believe in ghosts."

"I wasn't suggesting—"

"And yet, I feel like something is trying to reach across time and point something out to me—" Annie looked up sharply at Alice and laughed at herself. "OK. That sounds weird. I'm going to put the blame of all this spooky thinking on my empty stomach. How would you feel about going up to The Cup & Saucer? A lobster roll would cure all ailments right now."

9

The leisurely drive into town was soothing, and soon the break-in was almost forgotten. But as Alice and Annie parked behind the Cultural Center, they could see the ugly plywood boarding up the broken window.

Annie inhaled sharply. Shards of glass were still under the window and a piece of yellow crime tape clung to the side of the building.

"It's the yellow tape that makes it seem unreal," Annie said.

"Or too real," Alice added as she parked. The two women got out of the car to inspect closer. They walked around to the front and peered in the glass door. The museum was dark inside, but light filtered back from one of the inner offices. A sign on the door gave no explanation for the museum's closure: "Closed this morning. We plan to reopen at 2 p.m."

Alice looked at her watch. "They don't have too much time to prepare, do they?"

"But if it was only a little mischief ..."

"Right. Let's go eat and come back. Then we can get Hank to tell us the story. Oh, too late, he's waving at us from inside."

"You've heard?" he asked as he opened the door and gestured toward the broken window. Annie and Alice nodded as they stepped into the darkened interior of the Cultural Center. "The timing is just too coincidental," Hank continued, leading them toward the office in the back. "It's too early in the season for quote-unquote 'restless youth.' My grandson is that age, and all he can think about is skateboarding from morning to night. After a day of that, it's pizza and sleep that he wants." He turned and caught Annie's amused expression. She was about to speak, but he anticipated her skepticism. "No, no, no. Edwards is wrong on this one, Annie, I just know it."

"But why, Hank? Is the embroidery that valuable? You've shown that it's old, but even if it's some sort of collector's item, surely anyone who wanted it could have just approached one of us about buying it."

"Hmpf. And no one did last night, which is telling. Very telling." Annie failed to find such significance in this, but Hank was gesturing toward the display case holding the embroidered map. "Before we open this afternoon, we're working on enhancing the security. Annie, I hope you will continue to let us show the piece. I believe there is information out there in the memories of Stony Point citizens, and we should tap it before, ah, before ..." Hank's eyes darted about as if he expected another attempted break-in even as they stood there.

Privately, Annie still thought that Hank was overreacting, but she said, "I understand, Hank, and of course we'll keep the map on display. I have faith that you and Liz will do everything prudent to protect the exhibit." She clasped her hands and continued, "You look exhausted. Can't we entice you into joining us for lunch at The Cup & Saucer?"

"Oh no. Thank you, though. Too much to do here. Liz is out now picking up sandwiches, so ..." He slumped a bit as he spoke. Annie wondered if there was really a lot to do, or just a lot to worry about.

"Well, then, we shouldn't keep you. Do call if I can do anything, won't you?"

"Thank you, Annie. And I know I owe you an update on my research, which continues. Interesting stuff."

Without waiting to set a date to meet up with Hank again, who seemed too distracted to focus on his schedule anyway, Annie and Alice escaped into the warm sunshine of Main Street.

* * * *

The Cup & Saucer was abuzz with the energy of a lunch-time crowd on a gorgeous Saturday. Sunlight streamed in through the plateglass window, but its glare was softened by hanging baskets of ivy and flowering begonias. Threading their way through to an empty table, Annie and Alice nodded to a few patrons who had been at the exhibit the evening before.

They were shortly met by Peggy, who came over with an order form in her hand, but instead of asking whether they would like coffee, she pulled up an empty chair and exclaimed, "Can you believe it? It was so brazen! Practically in broad—well, OK, not really. But hardly under the cover of darkness, was it? I mean, that streetlight is practically right overhead. The nerve of some people!"

"Yes, well," Annie said. If she had any hopes of evading

prying questions, they were dashed now. "We don't actually know what happened, though."

"What do you mean? Someone smashed open the window, and Hank caught them in the act. Or not really caught, like with his bare hands," Peggy laughed, "but he foiled the attempt! It's just too bad he didn't have the presence of mind to take a picture just then." She stood and returned the chair she had sat in. "You gals want coffee? Do you want to order off the brunch menu?"

"Iced tea for me," Annie said, while Alice ordered a coffee.

"Coming right up. We have our daily specials on the chalkboard up on the wall. I'll describe anything to you when I come back with your drinks."

Annie took a cursory look at the menu, though by now she was famished, and she quickly settled on the lobster roll with coleslaw and baked beans. Alice had been swayed by the special of strawberry pancakes and maple syrup. The breezy chatter of the other patrons of the restaurant, punctuated by the clinks of forks and spoons against plates, reminded Annie of the restorative sounds of the ocean. Alice generously diverted Annie's attention from the map with questions about Annie's grandchildren in Texas and the progress of the shawl Annie was making for her daughter LeeAnn with the Two Ewe yarn. When Peggy brought their orders to the table, Annie and Alice were sketching out some ideas for coverlets to make for the next church bazaar.

Despite her best efforts to avoid the subject, however, Annie was regularly reminded of the map and the break-in by a trickle of friends and acquaintances who stopped by the table, eager to discuss the previous evening's excitement. Many seemed willing to entertain Hank's theory that the embroidery was the object of an attempted theft. One woman, whom Annie had met for the first time at the opening, expressed her dismay at the "crime wave" that Annie's discovery had brought to Stony Point. Annie couldn't quite make out if the woman was exaggerating or trying to be funny, but fortunately she had just taken a bite of lobster roll, and she gestured helplessly at her mouth. The woman seemed to take the hint graciously and moved on.

"Sounds like Hank has been busy," Alice observed with a smile.

"But what makes them think we would know more than the police at this point?" Annie wondered, shaking her head.

Alice shrugged, and before she could reply, Robert Stevens and his son Harry stopped at their table. Harry was Kate's estranged husband, and Annie's friendship with Kate sometimes made Annie feel a little uncomfortable around him. But Robert had a disarming smile that put people at ease in any situation.

"Having a nice repast, I see," Robert remarked, nodding his head. "It's been busy days for you, Annie, I hear."

"You mean the exhibition?" Annie said. "I didn't do any legwork for that, just loaned them what I found in my grandmother's attic."

"Quite a find too," Robert remarked. "After all these years."

Annie was startled by Robert's comment. "What do you mean? Do you know something about the embroidery?"

"Pop doesn't know anything about embroidery or stitch

work, unless it has to do with untangling fishing lines. Come on, old codger," Harry said, tugging on the sleeve of his dad's flannel shirt.

Robert flashed his son an odd smile. "Ah me," he sighed. "Time to go put my feet up on the couch and catch a game on TV." He tipped his ball cap in their direction and started toward the door.

Harry remained behind for a moment. "I saw the picture of it in the paper with the notice of the exhibit opening. Interesting." And with that cryptic remark he followed his father out onto the street.

10

Sunlight streamed through the windows of the Maine Folk Arts Center as Gus St. Pierre stood behind the display case, reading the latest issue of Maine Antique Digest. He looked up when the door opened, and for a moment he was dazzled by the sunlight and unable to make out the black figure silhouetted in the doorway; nevertheless, he felt a slight shiver travel up his spine.

After a moment, he cried, "Bucky? Is that you?"

The man stepped into the center, grinning. "As ever was. Except, nobody calls me that anymore." He stepped up to the other side of the display case but did not extend his hand.

Gus, whose expression of pleased recognition was already assuming a skeptical cast, automatically said, "Sorry." After a moment, he added, "What ... brings you to Maine?"

"Aw, you know. Old haunts. Memory lane." He spread his hands. "Family."

"I see." Gus's skeptical expression was becoming more firmly set. "How's ... Diane, is it?"

The man looked away. "She split," he said brusquely. "Took the kid."

"I'm sorry," Gus said. He started to add, "Are you in touch with them?" but the man spoke over his question.

"So these are Agnes's, huh?" He nodded in the direction of the artwork on the wall.

"Some of them, yes. This one," Gus jerked his thumb over his shoulder at the painting on the wall behind him, "and those over there."

"Nice, nice," the man said absently. "And have you seen her lately?"

"Not since last summer," said Gus. "She doesn't usually come up until after the Fourth of July. Past few summers, she's been spending less and less time in Maine."

The man nodded and seemed to come to some decision. "So the thing is," he said, "she offered to kinda, you know, give me one of these. Or, not the actual painting but the, you know, proceeds. She said I could maybe talk to you about getting an advance? Against the, you know, anticipated sale?" He gave the last two words an odd emphasis.

"Did she?" Gus asked mildly.

"Yeah," the man insisted, nodding and smiling. "Yeah, she did."

Gus pulled a cell phone out of his pocket. "Maybe we should just give her a call."

The man was instantly belligerent. "What, you don't trust me?"

Gus gazed at him levelly. "Trust you," he echoed. "I seem to recall a car battery that you sold me once. Only it turned out that it wasn't yours to sell."

"That was a long time ago," the man retorted. "We were just kids."

"You were seventeen," Gus said. "And I had to pay the rightful owner." He paused a moment and sighed. "I may not have seen Agnes for some months," he said, "but I talked to her on the phone just yesterday. She's had the boat put in, and I said I'd go up and check on it. We had a nice long conversation, and she didn't say a word about this. So ..." He held up the cell phone and began scrolling through its directory.

"OK, OK," the man said, gesturing for Gus to put the phone down. "I haven't ... asked her yet. But what's she gonna say? She's my sister after all."

Gus raised his eyebrows. "She may well say no." They locked eyes for a moment, until the man looked away and started to peer about the shop.

"Thing is ..." he said over his shoulder and then stopped as he picked up and examined a handblown glass plate that was on display under some hanging stained-glass window ornaments. "Thing is," he began again, "I gotta jump through hoops now just to see the kid. She's just about grown, don't you know. Diane's always wantin' money, saying she's gonna call her lawyer or her social worker or her mom." He laughed through gritted teeth. "Now there's a woman to put the fear of the devil in ya." He set the plate back down and turned around. Gus exhaled ever so quietly.

"I need money, Gus, for all the obvious reasons, and then some that ain't so obvious. I hate to bring up the past and bygones and all that, but ..." He let his words hang in the air while he stared at Gus.

Gus pursed his lips and narrowed his eyes, but after a moment, he sighed and shook his head sadly. He stepped to a small cash register set on a side table and rang it open. He slowly counted out some bills and set them on the counter in front of his visitor. "There's five hundred dollars. This is a loan, Bucky," he used the childhood nickname deliberately, "from me to you. Nothing to do with Agnes. And I will not loan you any more until this is paid back. Understood?"

"Sure, sure," the man was grinning again as he swept the bills off the counter. "From you to me," he added, leering at the till.

"It was my money to begin with," Gus said coldly. He glared at the man until the grin left his face.

"Yeah, OK," he muttered. "Thanks."

They stood in awkward silence for a moment, until Gus sighed again and said, "Well. Did you hear what happened to poor Davey?"

But this only seemed to make his visitor more agitated. "Yeah, yeah," he said, glancing toward the door. "Terrible. Just terrible. Listen, I gotta get going. Places to see, things to do, and all that." He started toward the door. "Thanks again for the ... loan." And he was gone.

Gus stared after him for a long time, a thoughtful expression on his face.

* * * *

The following Tuesday, Annie went, as usual, to the meeting of the Hook and Needle Club. She arrived to find the other members had already gathered.

"It's the celebrity!" cried out Mary Beth.

Annie stopped in her tracks to strike a glamour pose and then took her seat laughing. "You know, of course, that I didn't say most of those things," she said. "Or at least, not in the way they appeared."

The local newspaper, The Point, had run a feature on the attempted break-in at the Cultural Center and had decided to promote Hank's theory that the embroidered map was the target. Mike Malone, the publisher of the occasional paper, had called Annie to get her take on this possibility. She'd been happy to express her skepticism, but they'd had a long conversation, and by the time the story appeared in print, the truncated and out-of-context quotes gave the impression that she supported the theory.

"Annie," said Alice in a mockingly grave voice, "do you think you have acted responsibly in allowing the Historical Society to place this valuable artifact in such danger?"

"It's not her fault," said Peggy stoutly. "If she can't trust the Historical Society to look after such an important object, who can she trust?"

"You're right," Alice responded. "Clearly, she should have stuffed the thing back inside the clown and never allowed it to see the light of day."

Stella shook her head and muttered, "Such foolishness," which caused Alice and Peggy to laugh again.

"Well, I think Hank Page may be right," said Mary Beth. "After all, they must have been after something." She gave a decisive nod, wielding her knitting needles with extra vigor.

"But no, that's just the point, isn't it?" said Alice. "They may have just been out to make mischief, cause a little trouble. Like Chief Edwards says."

"Part of the problem," said Kate, "is that there's already a little mystery about the embroidery: Where did it come from? Who made it and why? What do those red Xs mean? If there weren't so many questions about the map itself,

I don't think people would be so quick to associate it with the break-in."

"Attempted break-in," Annie said automatically.

"Yes. Has there been more light shed on that, Annie?" asked Peggy.

Annie shook her head. "You all heard what Hank had to say at the reception. He hinted afterward that he knew a bit more than that. But then this all happened, and he hasn't told me any more about what he's learned. Or suspects. I got the impression he still isn't sure, whatever it is that he thinks."

"Didn't he say something about consulting an expert in Boston?"

"Yes, and I gather she's going to come up and see it, maybe later this week."

"Oh, you'll have to tell us what she says," exclaimed Kate. "I'm sure they'll have you there."

"They should consult you, Kate," said Mary Beth. "You're the one who figured out it was a map."

"Oh, but that was just a matter of looking at it. I wouldn't know anything about the history other than old stories the folks used to tell."

"I bet there's more to be learned just by looking," Alice said. "Like those red Xs. It seems like we ought to be able to figure out what those are or what they represent."

"Everyone in town is already trying," said Peggy. "It's the most popular topic at The Cup & Saucer. Theories range from lobster pots to buried treasure to alien abduction sites, but nobody's come up with anything that's totally convincing."

"Alien abductions!" said Stella.

"Well, OK, that was my contribution," said Peggy. "But

it sounded just as reasonable as all the others." She maintained a solemn expression for a few moments, but when Stella rolled her eyes, Peggy burst out laughing.

11

Annie had a full day ahead of her on Thursday already when she got a call from Gus St. Pierre in the morning. He complimented her again on the successful exhibit at the Cultural Center.

"It's a shame about the break-in." His tone of voice was sympathetic and not in the least prying. "Those things are disturbing, and violating, but vandalism—I'm sure it was nothing more than that—is a fact of life, unfortunately."

"Well, perhaps we are better off since we—the Historical Society, I mean—installed more security measures," Annie said, still trying to remain as neutral as possible.

"Yes, and that is good. And controversy can be good too. I hear the Cultural Center is seeing record attendance. But listen, I don't want to hold you up. I called because I can't help feeling that I'd like a little documentation of the embroidery piece for the Folk Arts Center; I have a few colleagues I would very much like to consult about it. I know you're committed to the Historical Society for the exhibit, but would you be willing to let me make a set of documentary photographs and some notes about the item? It would only take a day or so, and could even be done in situ at the museum, if necessary."

Annie briefly considered offering to send him the photo Hank took with his phone, but immediately she rejected that idea—it would not be of sufficiently high quality, she was sure. She said, "Gus, I'm happy to give you permission. Gosh, you hardly even need to ask. That is, so long as it doesn't interfere with the Historical Society's use. I'll call Liz to tell her it's OK; then I'll let you work out the logistics with her. But, Gus—" Annie hesitated, feeling suddenly a little tongue-tied on the phone with someone so versed in American arts and crafts.

"What is it, Annie?"

"I just wondered if you would share with me anything you are able to learn about the piece. I mean, it's so finely stitched, every detail just so. It's really remarkable."

"Naturally! I wouldn't think of leaving you out of the loop."

* * * *

Annie was a little relieved to find only Liz Booth at the Cultural Center when she arrived; she was scheduled to meet with Hank to learn about his research to date on the embroidery piece. As it happened, Hank's friend, the expert in historical textiles he had spoken of the night of the opening, was also coming up that morning, and Annie had been invited to sit in on her consultation. But Annie was glad to have a moment alone with Liz to explain to her about Gus's request to photograph the piece.

"Certainly, Annie," Liz assured her. "I have a lot of respect for Gus St. Pierre, and I know he's as careful in his research as Hank. True, Gus and Hank are rivals, and that is something that goes way back. But as historians,

I believe, they at least have a grudging respect for each other, despite a few ruffled feathers here and there." The two women stood over the case as if they were protecting the embroidery piece. It was an old, wooden case with a glass top, over which a dark cloth was draped. Liz pulled it back to show Annie the padlock on the box.

"At night—and this isn't information we are sharing widely—we have been removing the map from the display case and locking it in a fireproof safe we keep in the back office," Liz explained.

"I appreciate all this caution you are taking with the embroidery, but I wish it weren't necessary." Annie couldn't help, while the cloth was removed, gazing into the depths of the piece. "Well, I expect Gus will be calling you soon."

Liz smiled. "Actually, Annie, he already has." Liz looked down at the embroidered fabric. "There is something about this map that's significant. Both Hank and Gus sense it, but they aren't being very open about what they are thinking. They're too afraid that they'll be proven wrong and made fools of, I guess." She crossed her arms and smirked. "Men."

Just then they heard a knocking at the door, and they turned to see a strange woman holding a thick carpetbag. Liz replaced the cloth before unlocking the door and swinging it open to invite the woman in.

"I'm Emma James," the woman said without smiling, though she extended her hand. "I'm a conservator of vintage fabrics, here to meet Hank Page and look over his textile." She was petite and abrupt in the way she moved. Her black hair was styled in a sharply angled blunt cut that set off nicely her large, round black glasses.

"Oh yes! I'm Liz Booth, the president of the Historical Society. Do come in. Hank will be here in a few minutes." She drew the woman into the interior of the room and introduced her to Annie. "Annie, as I'm sure Hank explained, found the embroidery in her grandmother's attic."

"Pleased to meet you," Emma James said, shaking Annie's hand. "Hank didn't say much about how he came to be in possession of the piece, only that he thought it was interesting." Emma James's eye caught on the first display of aprons and recipes on the wall, and she wandered over to read the description. Then she scanned the entire room and took in the nature of the entire exhibit. "Wonderful," she said flatly. "I like what you've done here."

Emma James declined Liz's offer of a cup of tea while she waited for Hank. Instead, without turning around, she moved on to examine the next display. As she slowly circled the room, she asked Liz questions about local geography and industry, and some details about Stony Point's founding fathers and connection to maritime trade and inland logging camps. From her very specific questions, Annie felt that she'd learned more in ten minutes about the town's history and development than she had learned from her grandfather or from living in Stony Point.

"Excellent display, Ms. Booth," she said when she had finished her tour of the room with Liz and Annie at her heels.

"Please, do call me Liz."

"OK," the curator looked Liz in the eyes and said. "You can call me Emma James." There was an awkward pause before she explained, "My cousin and I have the same first name, so I've always been called Emma James. It's like my first name now." Then she smiled for the first time. "Hank is late," she continued, looking up at the clock on the wall. "Perhaps you can show me the embroidery, Liz. And Annie, I would like to hear your story about finding it."

As Liz went about removing the embroidery piece from its case, Emma James opened her bag and pulled out a small, plain notepad and a pen. She opened the pad to a fresh piece of paper and carefully laid the pen down on a diagonal so that it pointed to the first line of the paper. She next pulled out a pair of white cotton gloves, a large magnifying apparatus, and a piece of plain muslin, which she spread on top of the case before setting the embroidery piece on it. The large, round magnifying glass was set into a black frame with a light that circled the glass; it was attached by a jointed arm to a base on which the object of study could be placed.

She had pulled on the gloves and was engrossed in examining the piece when Hank came barreling in.

"Emma James! So good to see you! I'm so sorry I'm late. I had a flat on my way in. Liz, do you know your cell phone isn't turned on? I've been trying to call. Oh look, you've started. Amazing, isn't it?"

"Hank." Emma James looked up briefly, giving her second smile of the morning. Her gloved hands remained on the magnifying glass. "Everything is OK with the car, I hope."

"Yes, just a flat, after all, but annoying. Annie, finally, my dear, we have an opportunity to talk about this … this map!"

Emma James returned to her magnifying glass. She began to talk as she scanned the fabric.

"I commend you all on the care you have taken with the piece. You've done everything right. The colors are brilliant, which suggests to me that this piece has not seen much of the light of day." She set aside her magnifier and flipped over the muslin, paying as much attention to the back as she did the front. "Aha," she said. Hank, Liz, and Annie waited for her to say more, but she was silent for a long two minutes as she scribbled a notation on her notepad. Annie and Liz glanced at one another, but Hank seemed unperturbed. Annie, uncomfortable with the silence, was about to mention again that the piece had been stuffed into the cookie jar when the expert resumed her discussion.

"See this," Emma James pointed with her gloved finger to a faint orange mark near the corner. "Look closely at the hem, and you can see a 'maker's mark.' This is an identifying mark that we sometimes see on the selvage of fabrics. It can tell us who made this piece of muslin, if not who made the map itself.

"If I had this in my workshop at the museum, I would gently undo the hem, here, to examine the mark more thoroughly. But just from my examination with the glass, I can see that it appears to be a part of the trademark symbol of a mill near Brunswick. And since we know, or can find out, when that mill was operating, this may help us determine when the fabric was made, and thus help us narrow down when the piece was made and whether the artist was local."

After Hank, Liz, and Annie had a chance to look through the magnifier at the maker's mark, Emma James flipped and recentered the embroidery piece. She resumed her scrutiny of the stitch work. "It's hard to see with the naked eye," she said after a moment, "but if you look through the glass you see an interesting pattern of frayed threads running horizontally here and vertically here, which suggests to me that someone at one time had folded this piece up like a sheet of paper."

"To store it?" suggested Liz.

"Possibly, but if so, it must have had quite a lot stored on top of it, because the wear suggests that the fabric was significantly compacted while folded." She turned to Annie. "Was it tightly folded when you found it?"

"No, quite loosely folded. Sort of half rolled, half folded."

Emma James nodded, cocking her head and squinting through the glass. "Yes, I think this was done some time ago. Also, it appears to have been folded down to quite a small size, smaller than would seem necessary to fit it in a drawer. I think it may be more likely that it was folded to be carried, perhaps in a pocket or packed tightly in a suitcase. But that seems rather strange."

"Why is that?" Annie asked.

"It's a decorative object," Hank said. "It was made to be displayed in some way, probably hung on a wall."

"So why would anyone need to carry it about so much?" muttered Emma James. She stepped back to allow the others to look again through the magnifier.

"I hadn't noticed that at all," Annie said, shaking her head as she stepped back from her turn.

"No, you wouldn't—not without equipment and probably not unless you knew to look for it. But patterns of wear are among the things I look for in assessing fabric." Emma

James pushed the muslin out from under the magnifying glass and moved the contraption over to the side of the case.

"Note the different stitches."

Annie and Liz nodded. Hank bent and looked closer as if he was just now noticing the stitch work.

"There's some variety, but I wouldn't jump to the conclusion that the stitching patterns indicate more than one person worked on the piece. Around the turn of the century, needlework was a popular pastime for women with a certain amount of leisure. Needlework periodicals or pamphlets were also gaining popularity and were inspiring women to try new stitch work. So it's not impossible to find various stitches in the work of a single woman.

"Another thing. Note the way the older matte embroidery thread is used with the mercerized cotton threads, which have a bit of sheen to them. The person who created this map used the juxtaposition of flat and shiny threads to heighten the effects of shading and depth. That suggests a degree of sophistication at the conceptual level. In my opinion, it further supports the notion that this would be the work of a single individual."

Emma James set the cloth down and began packing up her magnifying glass. She helped Liz reposition the muslin in the display case before removing her white gloves, but her thoughts were still on the differences in the threads. "The artist used the contrast between the two types of threads the way a painter would work with color and tone. That suggests not just an artistic eye, but also extensive experience in needlecrafts. And of course, the elegance of the execution also bears that out." She paused. "I think the key to understanding where this piece came from is these letters YSP, whatever they might stand for."

Emma James stared down at the embroidery for another moment, as if trying to confirm her conclusions. Then she turned away and closed up her carpetbag.

"We could do a thorough fiber and chemical analysis in my lab at the museum," she said, straightening up. "There are, I'm sure, many more hidden details that would help us understand its history. Bits of grit or hair can tell you a lot." Emma James picked up her bag and stepped a few paces toward the door as she spoke. Stopping and turning, she said, "I do feel that you have a remarkable piece. It's fairly old and should have a lot to say, with further investigation. I would strongly urge you to bring it down to me or take it to some other museum or conservator's workshop for more analysis."

Annie suddenly realized that all eyes were on her. "Yes, I would like that, but—well, I feel that it really needs to be displayed here, for the people of Stony Point, at least for the time being."

"But, Emma James," Liz broke in, "you've said nothing about the red Xs or the numbers written on the back. What can you tell us about those?"

"Nothing at this point," she said simply. Then she pulled out her business card for Liz and Annie, shook Hank's hand, picked up her carpetbag, and left.

* * * *

The sound of Emma James's heels as she left the Cultural Center was still clicking in Annie's head as Liz set down three mugs of hot water and a selection of black, green, and herbal teas. She watched Hank stir two heaping spoonfuls of sugar into his black tea and waited eagerly for him to begin with his response to the new information. She resisted the urge to prompt him.

"Well," he said finally, clinking his spoon back and forth in his mug, trying to cool the tea a little, "Emma James's speculations don't contradict what people have been telling me. I no longer think that this was produced in piecework by various hands. And I don't think there is more than one—set of hands, that is. I think this is an artisan's creation." Hank stared into his mug and then took a tentative sip of the tea, wincing as if it were bitter. "I have my suspicions too about that YSP, though I haven't wanted to say anything about that yet."

As Annie listened, she held her mug of hot tea to her lips and blew over the top to cool it. When Hank mentioned that last bit, she jostled her tea and managed to burn her lips.

"That's a huge step forward, Hank. What?"

"A couple of women ran a seaside trading post just north of here in the twenties and thirties. Sisters. One was something of an artist, painter, but never really flourished—I s'pose family and work got in the way. Her name was Yvette St. Pierre."

"St. Pierre? Any chance she is a relation to Gus St. Pierre?" Liz asked.

"The two sisters, Yvette and Marie, ran the trading post till it blew down in a hurricane in the late thirties, I believe. Interesting ladies. Eccentric, I should say."

Annie took a more cautious sip this time. "No wonder

Gus is so interested. If he has a family connection to the piece … I wonder if he will try to claim it."

"I wondered that too," Hank said. "There's certainly no record of whose hands it's passed through. Typical of the St. Pierres."

"You sound like you know quite a bit about the family." Annie hated to probe, but she was starting to lose patience with Hank's evasiveness, and a little confidence in him too.

Hank leaned forward with his elbows on the table and steepled his fingers. "I s'pose I know more about the family than most folks in these parts."

Liz gasped and suddenly compared her watch to the clock on the wall. "I'd completely forgotten about the time. We're supposed to open to the public in just a few minutes." She stood and started collecting the tea things, but Annie elbowed her out of the way.

"I'll wash up, Liz," she said. She reached for Hank's half-empty mug. He didn't seem to notice the commotion around him. He was staring up at the ceiling, rubbing his chin, lost in thought.

12

Annie's next appointment on Thursday was with Mary Beth. They'd arranged to meet up at her shop before heading out for lunch with Laura Coyne. As Annie was running a little late, she made an ill-considered decision to jaywalk across Main Street and promptly heard a screech of tires. Startled, Annie jumped, but what cars there were midmorning were moving very slowly and mostly looking for parking spaces. She hastily made her way to the other side of the street when the owner of the screeching tires came into view. It was none other than the goateed man in his battered van.

Annie slipped into A Stitch in Time and nearly bumped into Mary Beth, who apparently had her purse already on her arm and was worried about being late for their lunch date with Laura.

"It's him," Annie blurted out, by way of greeting. "Look!"

"You sure?"

The two women cracked the door of the shop, letting out cool air, and craned their necks around. The dark-haired man was just that moment stamping out a cigarette on the sidewalk.

Mary Beth straightened up and stepped outside. "We have a trash can, you know!" The man looked up at her, a little surprised at being addressed, but trying not to show it.

Mary Beth pointed at a spot just beyond the van. "Right behind you."

"Sorry, lady," the stranger said, sauntering past the shop, not stopping to pick up his cigarette butt.

Undeterred, Mary Beth followed him. "Young man, would you mind if I asked you a question? What were you doing at the site of the house fire on Elm Street?"

"Lady, I do mind, and it's none of your business no how." The goateed man gave Mary Beth a hard stare, then spat on the ground and continued on, leaving Mary Beth, for once, speechless and feeling not in charge.

Annie sidled up to Mary Beth and slipped her arm in hers. "Come on," she urged gently. "We're late for our lunch." Mary Beth let Annie lead her in the opposite direction, toward where her car was parked on the street. Annie threw a parting glance over her shoulder, expecting to see the back of the goateed man, but instead she saw him leaning against another car, watching her. When she met his eyes, he gave her a lazy salute and a nod, as if to say, "I know who you are."

* * * *

The "color intervention" had done wonders for the Coynes' tiny apartment. When Annie and Mary Beth arrived, Laura Coyne had a new tablecloth spread over the Formica kitchen table, hiding its somewhat rusty legs. The clown cookie jar was set on the counter so it was the first thing that greeted you when you entered the kitchen.

Laura had been inspired to do some thrift shopping,

and she had picked up a tiered cut-glass tray on which she'd arranged cucumber and cream cheese sandwiches cut into triangles on the middle tier, with grapes and cheese on top, and cupcakes on the bottom for dessert. At the same thrift shop, she'd also picked up a variety of small bud vases, which now dotted the kitchen with small clumps of wild pansies and Johnny jump-ups.

Annie could see the delight on Mary Beth's face when she saw the transformation of the apartment. *It's just what I needed to see too,* she thought.

"My cousin Eileen picked up the kids and took them to Boston, so while they've been away I've had a little time to fix up the place and to start to feel more at home," Laura explained when the women were at the table. "It's supposed to be a vacation for us as much as for the kids, but Eileen's idea of a vacation is chamber music and museums. Megan will have a blast, but Martin I'm afraid is a little too young to sit still for a lot of cultural things. So far, though, she hasn't sent him home early, so he must be behaving."

"I loved being the grand aunt to my niece—all the special things we could do together," Mary Beth mused. Annie suppressed a little pang of regret for living so far away from her grandchildren.

"And it has been a vacation for us too," Laura went on. "Old friends of David's from his fishing days dropped by when they heard about the fire and brought us a couple of lobsters and a big, old pot to boil them in." She patted her stomach and laughed. "And the kids feel bad because they think we just die of boredom when they are away with Eileen."

“I didn’t know David had been a fisherman,” Mary Beth said.

“Used to be. He’d go out for weeks at a time, but he gave that up when the kids came along. Doesn’t miss it one whit, he says.”

Annie smiled and bit into her sandwich. Her taste buds were awakened with the infusion of dill and arugula, cream cheese, and cucumber. “Delicious, Laura!”

Laura blushed. “Well, I hoped you’d like it. I’d love to do a luncheon for the whole Hook and Needle Club at one of your meetings.”

“Lovely idea!” Mary Beth said. “Let’s wait until Megan can join us. The ladies are so eager to meet her.”

Mary Beth and Laura started working out when the luncheon would be, but ran into a number of scheduling conflicts as Laura and David were meeting with contractors and filing permits and such to rebuild their home.

“If, that is, we can ever get this ‘arson’ thing settled.” Laura sighed. “Chief Edwards and Chief Besham have been low-key about it, thank goodness. I don’t believe they think we would have set fire to our own house, but they can’t seem to figure out how it did happen. They say it started in the basement, but there’s no ‘obvious ignition source.’ I don’t see how it could have, myself; it’s just a crawl space down there.” She inhaled sharply. “Or was, I mean. Ah, me …” Laura flexed her hands; they’d been balled into fists as she spoke.

“Dear, I know things are going to work out soon enough. The important thing is not to lose faith during the process. You have a lot of good people on your side.”

"I know that." Laura smiled as she recovered her composure. "Would either of you like coffee with dessert? You've probably guessed that I worked in a bakery at one time. In college." She stood and began to bustle about the kitchen, talking as if to distract herself. "And I considered—still do, in fact—going to culinary school. You know, if that's one thing that's come out of this mess, it's that David and I had a long talk about dreams and what we'd like to do. David would like to own his own garage one day, and I dream about managing a little tea shop, with old-fashioned dishes and a simple menu of finger foods."

"And you can think of the Hook and Needle Club luncheon as building a customer base. I love it!" Mary Beth's voice bounced around the tiny kitchen and changed the tenor of the conversation, but just for a minute.

As Mary Beth and Annie waited for coffee, they happily sampled the cupcakes and cookies—applesauce ginger with lemon cream icing, and chocolate with orange mocha icing. As they ate, however, the worried crease on Laura's brow began to reappear.

Annie sensed that she still wanted to talk about the fire, so she ventured a question. "There's more going on, isn't there, than just the fire?"

Laura looked up and tears welled up in her eyes. "Yes," she whispered. "If only it were just the fire." She dabbed her eyes with the corner of her napkin.

"You see, David's cousin ... he showed up out of the blue in ... February, I think it was. He wanted to borrow money. Then he didn't think he should have to pay it back, something about David's mother inheriting the house. Then he turned up again a few weeks ago, and he's been coming back off and on, always wanting a place to stay. Thank goodness he wasn't here when we had the fire. But now he claims that he should get a share of the insurance money—money that we haven't even seen yet! We just don't need any more drama right now."

Laura balled her hands into fists and then flexed them out again.

"This cousin," Annie asked. "Is he a dark-haired man with a goatee and tattoos on his arms?"

"Lionel. Yes, that's him. Ugh!"

Annie shot Mary Beth a look, and Mary Beth nodded in return.

"You don't think he could have had something to do with starting the fire, do you?" Mary Beth asked. To Annie the question felt intrusive, though she had to admit to herself that she was thinking along the same lines.

Laura stood up abruptly and started making coffee. It seemed to give her something to do. "I can't believe Lionel would go that far. I don't think he would mean us any real harm." The emotion in her voice was obvious. "But Lionel is, well, careless and ... well, he's not my cousin; he's David's, and I try not to speak ill of his family. They're a tight-knit bunch. Or had been. I think the cousins are starting to drift apart."

Laura brought over mugs—Annie recognized one that came from the yard-sale box—and cream and sugar. "What's missing? Oh, spoons!" She turned away to grab some more flatware, and with her back to Annie and Mary Beth, Laura continued talking. "And some of his other family have been wonderful. Another cousin that we haven't seen much lately has been very supportive. He bought the kids all new clothes. Shoes, backpacks ... he said they shouldn't have to look poor in front of the other kids." She returned to the table with the spoons and sat down.

Then she looked at them in confusion, "Did you say you wanted coffee?" They assured her that they had.

* * * *

Annie's head was spinning by the time Mary Beth and Annie got back in the car and headed for home. She wanted to work her thoughts out with Mary Beth, but she was afraid that voicing her thoughts might somehow make the situation worse. She simply couldn't believe that the Coynes could have set fire to their own house, and she was dismayed to hear that such an investigation was still proceeding.

"Mary Beth ..." Annie started to say, but her companion spoke simultaneously, and louder.

"Annie," she said. "Annie, we've got to help them get to the bottom of this!"

"Them who?"

"The Coynes, the police. Perhaps we should go right now to tell them about our suspicions about this cousin Lionel."

"But you already reported seeing him at the house after the fire."

"But I didn't know who he was then!" Mary Beth quickly protested.

Annie spoke as soothingly as she could. "No, but I would

bet that Chief Edwards could put a name to the description you gave him, and since this Lionel hasn't been arrested, we can assume that he had an alibi that checks out."

"Humpf," Mary Beth said, mulling over what Annie said. "Humpf," she repeated.

"I think the more important question might be *why*. Why would someone want to burn down David Coyne's house?"

"Why indeed, why indeed?" Mary Beth's voice was brought down to a whisper, and she drove the rest of the way back to Grey Gables with a pensive expression on her face.

13

"What was *that*?"

Annie sat bolt upright in bed, gasping as her mind leaped in a single bound from deepest sleep to full alert. She groped with her left hand to shake Wayne awake as her wide-open eyes darted about the dark room. Even in the gloom, she could tell things weren't right: The dim light was wrong, the loom and bulk of the shadows were strange. Her hand found only bedclothes. Where was …?

Her whole body sagged. He was gone, of course. And she wasn't home in Brookfield, but rather she was alone in the large bedroom of Grey Gables in Maine.

She was pierced by the full force of the grief that had struck her when Wayne died, and she sat, clutching the empty sheets and blankets beside her, unconscious of her surroundings or the passing of time.

Eventually she gave a small, rueful laugh. As far as she could remember, this was a cliché that they had never enacted in life: the wife waking the husband to demand he investigate some noise in the night. Of course, he would have done so to set her mind at rest, though what Wayne Dawson, that gentlest of men, would have done if he had actually encountered an intruder, Annie could not imagine.

For a while after Wayne's death, Annie had suffered from nightmares. She would wake from dreams in which something terrible was about to happen to her husband, only to realize afresh that something terrible had. But she'd not had such a dream in a long time now, and besides, it wasn't a dream that woke her this time, she felt sure of that.

So what had it been? Some noise, undoubtedly. This old house, exposed to the persistent coastal winds, was much more talkative than her house in Brookfield. It groaned and moaned and complained almost constantly. I'll probably do much the same, Annie thought, when I reach a comparable age. But still, she had thought she'd grown accustomed to the house's noises. She refocused on her senses, peering again into the gloom and listening intently. She heard nothing untoward.

Slowly she began to relax. She laid her head back down and allowed her mind to drift, thinking of all she'd learned recently about needlework and the map.

Then she heard a noise.

Annie caught her breath and listened so intently she thought she could hear the draft of air in the room. She was already trying to tell herself that it was nothing, just another of the house's complaints. But the other part of her mind knew this was not the case; whatever she'd heard, it was not one of the usual noises of the night.

And then it came again.

It was some sort of muffled thump. It was definitely coming from within the house, downstairs. She tried to imagine some cause other than a person moving about down there, but her adrenaline had already spiked in fight-or-flight, and she couldn't concentrate. Her heart thumped in her chest and her breath came in short, shallow gasps. She lay paralyzed, torn between the two instinctual responses.

This will not do, she admonished herself sternly. She forced herself to close her eyes and take some deep breaths. Then she considered her options.

Call for help? She had no telephone extension upstairs, and her cell phone was also downstairs. *Well, there is a lesson for the future*, she thought.

Hide upstairs? If the intruder were a burglar, he might or might not come upstairs, but she thought he probably would, seeking jewelry or cash, and he might find her. If the intruder meant her harm, he would search until he found her. In either case, if she were found hiding, she'd be in a defensively weak position. Besides, she wasn't sure she had the nerve to just sit and wait. She felt the need to take some sort of action.

Confront the intruder? Even if she had a weapon—and she couldn't think of one that was handy—a confrontation would probably be more dangerous for her than for him. Backing a desperate person into a corner was never a good idea. But suppose she didn't confront him directly, but just made a lot of noise coming down the stairs? She thought the chances were good that he would simply flee, given the chance. Unless he were there specifically to do her harm, but she couldn't imagine who would want to do so.

And what about flight? Perhaps she could sneak down the stairs and out the door herself, and then call the police from Alice's. The danger was that she might surprise the intruder on her way out.

Suddenly Annie felt she could not sit still any longer. She didn't feel confident about scaring the intruder off, so escaping the premises seemed the best option. She threw off her sheet and blanket, and cautiously placed her feet on the floor. She stood slowly, dreading a floorboard creak, and then froze at the sound of another muffled thump from downstairs. She felt her carefully cultivated calm dissolve in a fresh wave of adrenaline. It seemed to her that the sound had come from the dining room directly below her, but she strained to catch any evidence of someone stealthily climbing the stairs. Nothing.

Releasing her held breath, Annie looked down at her flannel pajamas. She could pluck her robe from the chair as she passed by, but if she planned to sneak outside, she would need something for her feet. She sat back down on the bed and pulled on some sneakers without bothering with socks. She was moving more quickly now, perhaps too quickly, but her fright, which she had only temporarily stifled, was rising again and threatening to overwhelm her.

She stepped to the chair for her heavy terry-cloth robe and almost panicked completely when one arm caught in the sleeve as she tried to draw it on. She tied the sash and then forced herself to move slowly toward the open door of the bedroom. She stood at the threshold, listening hard for any sound from the floor below. Her heart skipped at the merest creak, and the sound of her furnace coming on almost made her cry aloud, but she heard nothing that was definitely the sound of the intruder. Perhaps he'd already gone?

Standing in the door, she suddenly felt very exposed, and she tried again to think of something in her bedroom that she might use as a weapon. Nothing came to mind. She paused a moment longer, fearing that once she took a step, she'd be unable to keep herself from bolting down the stairs. Then she moved forward cautiously.

She was halfway to the top of the stairs when she heard the sound of stealthy footsteps that were not her own. She froze and listened. The intruder was moving along the downstairs hallway from the back of the house to the front. *After he'd finished in the dining room, he must have moved back to the family room or the library*, she thought. Would he have wasted any time in the kitchen? She certainly had nothing valuable there, but how would he have known? A hope flared in her heart: Perhaps he was heading toward the door! But no; is a burglar going to exit the house by the front door?

She could no longer hear the footsteps. Had he stopped? Annie thought that he had turned into the living room, but she couldn't be sure. If so, this put him closer to her route of escape. Her fright began to get the better of her. She was sure that he had almost finished ransacking the first floor and would soon be making his way to the second. If she didn't hurry, she'd end up meeting him on the stairs! However long it took him to search the living room for valuables was the time she had to get down the stairs and out the door.

She was moving again before she even realized it, stealing swiftly to the top of the stairs. Without pausing, she began to quickly descend. She'd intended to test each step on her way down, but fear was now driving out caution. As she descended, she kept eyes and ears fixed on the door to the living room. She could definitely hear him moving around in there now, though he was apparently taking care to be quiet. But the certainty that he was in the living room only further spurred her fear. If he stepped out of the room now, he would stand between her and the front door. She would have to turn and race down the hall to the back door, pursued by the intruder.

Thoroughly frightened, she flew from the foot of the stairs to the front door. She'd forgotten that she would need to work the lock before she could open the door, but fortunately, her hands flew automatically to turn the handle and dead bolt. In the split second it took to unlock the door, she cast an involuntary glance into the living room, where she spied a dark shape at the far end that had just turned her way in apparent surprise.

For a moment, time seemed to stop. She couldn't make out features, but the man's silhouette stood out against the light filtering through the window curtains. The shadowy figure stood slightly crouched, his head cocked to one side. She was sure he was staring at her. To Annie, he seemed like a cat ready to spring. She gasped, breaking the horrible silence of the frozen moment.

And then she threw open the door and raced onto the porch, down the steps, and away from the house.

* * * *

Two hours later Annie sat with a mug of tea in Alice's kitchen. The police cruiser in front of her own house no longer strobed its blue lights, but it was still parked there and the officers were still inside, checking the premises.

"I should have just stayed and confronted him." Annie

had been second-guessing her actions almost since she had arrived.

"That would have been foolish," Alice repeated, beginning to sound impatient.

Contrite, Annie said again, "I'm sorry." She'd given Alice a considerable fright when she burst into the house. Annie had remembered that Alice usually kept her back door unlocked, and when the intruder had spotted her fleeing the house, Annie had been sure she'd be pursued. So rather than ring Alice's doorbell as she'd intended, she'd come rushing in the back door yelling for Alice to call the police. In fact, Annie had called them herself by the time Alice got over her own shock and fright enough to understand what was happening.

Alice gave a tired smile. "It's certainly a change of pace," she said, sipping her tea. "How are you feeling?"

Once the police had been called, and it seemed clear that the intruder had not followed her to Alice's house, Annie had trembled uncontrollably for some time. That had now passed, and she felt very tired. But she'd promised to stay up and talk with the police some more so there was no going to bed yet. Alice had already made it clear that Annie would spend the rest of the night with her.

"There's no need for you to stay up, though," Annie said, repeating an earlier remark, but Alice declined to give the same response this time, and merely shrugged.

After a few moments, Alice began asking Annie about her grandchildren. She didn't elicit any information that she hadn't already heard, but she knew it was a topic that could divert Annie's thoughts from the night's events. Soon, however, Reed Edwards knocked at the door.

"Chief Edwards," said Annie with concern, "I'm so sorry, I didn't realize they would get you out of bed for this."

"Not to worry," the chief said, shaking his head. "I was already up." He lifted his travel mug of coffee toward Alice to decline her offer of something to drink. "I know you've been through it all with Officer Peters, but I'd appreciate it if you could just tell it to me again." Annie resumed her seat at the table while the chief pulled out his notebook.

When she had finished, the chief said, "So you saw the intruder?"

"Just a glimpse. I was more concerned about him seeing me."

"But you're sure it was a man? Can you tell me anything else about him?"

"Yes, it was definitely a man, but I saw him more as a shadow than anything." Annie closed her eyes and tried to recall what she'd seen. What came to her most vividly was the figure's posture—frozen, alert, in a predatory hunch. But this didn't seem useful for police purposes.

After a moment, she tried, "Not too tall, I would say. Average build? He didn't seem to be either fat or extraordinarily skinny. I guess he seemed pretty … solid. His clothes may have been dark, but that could have been, you know," she opened her eyes and gave him a wry look, "the absence of light."

"Hair color?" the chief prompted. "Skin color? Facial hair? Age?"

But Annie shook her head. "Too dark."

Chief Edwards made some further notes, and then narrowed his eyes at her. "What do you think they were after?"

Annie shrugged. "What are burglars ever after? Cash? Jewelry? Electronic equipment? I don't have much like that in the house." She looked at Alice as if seeking her opinion. "I've got some antiques that are probably worth some money, things of my grandmother's. But would a burglar go for something like that? I'd think you'd have to have time and expertise to steal that kind of stuff." Alice nodded in agreement. "Did he ... make much of a mess upstairs? Did he go into the attic?"

The chief shook his head. "We found drawers pulled out and things messed about downstairs, especially in the back rooms, but nothing appears to be disturbed upstairs. We think the burglar may have fled when he saw you."

"Chasing me?" Annie asked with alarm.

"We think he both entered and left by the back door; you came out the front. There seem to be tracks, but we'll know better in daylight. No, we think you spooked him as much as he spooked you, so he ran when he saw you. Amateurs will usually take off at the first sign of trouble. And even if he didn't panic outright, he probably figured you'd be calling the police."

"You're sure it was an amateur?" Alice asked.

"Annie never would have heard him, otherwise," said the chief. "Besides," he added, "Stony Point isn't the kind of place to attract professionals. But Annie, are you sure you can't think of anything specific that the thief might have been after?"

Annie gave him a sharp look. "What are you getting at, Chief? What's going on?"

Chief Edwards sighed. "Well, it's just that this wasn't the

only break-in last night." Both women looked at him in amazement. "Sometime before this intruder entered your house, Annie, somebody broke into the Cultural Center once again, and this time they made it inside without interruption." He looked to see how they were taking this news, but both seemed surprised and puzzled. "And this time, it's clear what they were after: The case that held that embroidered map had been tipped over, but nothing else had been touched. I think the thief may have kicked it over when he saw that the map wasn't there."

"So you think he was after the map after all?" Alice exclaimed in amazement.

"But it wasn't there," Annie quickly protested. "They've been locking it up in a safe at night."

The chief nodded slowly. "That's right, and it's still there, safe and sound. But the point is, not many people knew they were doing that."

Alice was quicker to the mark. "So you think whoever it was assumed that Annie had taken the map back to her own house, and that's what he was after!"

14

The next day Annie went through her house with Officer Peters to confirm that nothing was missing.

Boots the cat met them at the door, complaining loudly about the disruption of the nighttime routine. Annie felt absurdly glad to see her and rather guilty because she'd given the cat no thought in her flight from the house the night before. Alice went to the kitchen to feed her and then caught up with Annie and the police officer as they made a systematic examination of the house.

Annie found two levels of mess: that made by the thief as he had apparently searched for the map and that made by the police technicians as they had dusted for fingerprints and searched for other clues. Peters gave Annie an apologetic look. "Crime can be a messy business, I'm afraid."

But Annie could not find anything missing. "If he was after the map—" she began.

Peters shrugged. "If he came across cash or jewelry, he might seize his opportunity even if he were here for the map," he said. "But the fact that nothing seems to be missing strongly suggests that he was after something specific, and our best candidate for that is this … embroidery." If Peters felt any skepticism about the notion that someone would break into a house just to steal a piece of needlework, his carefully neutral tone did not betray it.

Annie's shoulders sagged. "I wish now I'd never found it."

Alice, trailing them through the house, put her arm around Annie's shoulders and squeezed. "Come on then," she said, "let's get this cleaned up."

Annie looked at Peters. "Is it OK to …" She gestured at the mess in the family room.

The officer nodded. "We've learned all we can from the scene," he said, but appeared to regret his use of the word when he saw Annie stiffen. In a softer voice, he said, "Are you … planning to stay here tonight? We'll have a watch on the house, you know. Though it's very unlikely that he'll be back."

"She's staying with me," Alice said decisively. "For a few days, at least," she added with a meaningful look at Annie. Though she'd previously insisted that one night away would be sufficient, Annie felt defeated by the mess she saw around her, and now she nodded in mute acquiescence. "We'll clean this up and pack you some clothes," Alice continued briskly, "and then we'll go grocery shopping. We're going to cook something special this evening as a means of putting this behind us. And you," she added, looking down at Boots, who was twining around their ankles, "can stay at whichever house you like."

* * * *

In fact, they decided to do the shopping first and come back to clean up the house in the afternoon. Alice thought Annie needed a break and some other activity before further reminders of the night's frightening events. They decided on vegetable lasagna and set out for Magruder's to lay in supplies.

Magruder's Groceries was directly across Main Street from the Cultural Center, and as they pulled into the store's parking lot, they couldn't help but notice that the recently repaired back window was now once again covered by a piece of plywood. Annie gazed at it for a long moment, but said nothing.

Inside the grocery store, they ran into Hank Page, who was shuffling through the aisles with one of the store's baskets on his arm. "Just trying to get caught up on my marketing," he said with a tired smile. "I've been too busy lately to attend to the household necessities." His voice grew grave. "Have you heard?" he asked with a gesture of his head toward the Cultural Center.

Alice looked at Annie to take her cue. "Oh, we've heard," Annie said. "We've more than heard." Hank's face showed his confusion, and Annie explained about the break-in at her own house. As she told her story, Hank's face became suffused with anger.

"That infernal rat!" he exclaimed. "How dare he?"

His response startled Annie, and Alice cried, "You know who it was?"

Hank drew breath to respond but then hesitated. "Well, I think I've got a pretty good idea," he said angrily. He calmed a bit as he added, "Though Chief Edwards does think I'm jumping to conclusions."

They waited a moment for him to continue, until finally Alice couldn't stand it. "Well, who do you think it is?"

"Gus St. Pierre," Hank replied solemnly.

"But why?" Annie asked at last.

"Look at the interest he's shown in that map," Hank said eagerly. "You yourself said he wanted to borrow it from you when you went to ask him about it. And I saw how he acted the night of the reception. I've thought all along it's him. I think he's dying to get his hands on it."

"But why would he try to steal it when he's coming to photograph it?" Annie demanded. Hank look startled, and she explained, "Gus called me the other day. He wanted permission to make a set of documentary photographs of the map. I said it was fine with me so long as it didn't interfere with the Historical Society's work. I was very clear that the Society had priority," she emphasized, as Hank started to bristle, "so he called Liz, and they worked out a schedule that accommodates everyone. I believe he'll be taking them sometime next week." She paused and watched this sink in. "So why would he take the risk of trying to steal it when he's already arranged to take these pictures? Won't they be just as useful to him as the actual embroidery?"

"Hmm, well, of course pictures aren't the same as possession," Hank said, but Annie could hear the conviction leaking out of his voice. "Still, as you say, that does cast a new light on things. Hmm ..." He sighed. "Well, if it's not Gus—and I'm not yet fully persuaded of that, mind you—but if it's not, then who on earth is it?"

* * * *

Annie and Alice loaded up on pasta, spinach, tomatoes, portabella mushrooms, onions, and fresh mozzarella and ricotta cheeses for the lasagna, plus biscotti and ice cream for after dinner, but when they were done, Annie rejected Alice's suggestion of lunch at The Cup & Saucer. "It may not have reached Hank yet, but I'm sure the story is traveling all over town," Annie said. The grapevine was so much more efficient in these small New England towns than it had been back in Brookfield. "I don't think I'm quite ready yet for the sympathy and interrogations."

So they returned to Alice's house for a quiet lunch of tea and sandwiches, and then they made their way back to Grey Gables to clean up the mess and pack some clothes for Annie. A police car was prominently parked across the street from the house, and Annie looked at it with both relief and puzzlement. "Surely Chief Edwards can't keep that car there all day," she said. But the officer who waved to them as they approached the door to the house seemed settled in for his vigil.

They had stocked up on cleaning supplies at the grocery store, and Alice now drew out the large sponges with which they planned to attack the black fingerprint powder. "Why don't you go upstairs and pack, and I'll get a start on the cleanup."

Annie hesitated before nodding. She hated to foist this chore off onto Alice, but just the sight of the mess was starting to oppress her spirits once again, and she didn't think she was quite yet up for the cleaning. Slowly, she climbed the stairs and made her way down the hall to her bedroom door. The sense of oppression continued to grow, and as she stood outside the room, alone for the first time in many hours, she felt an echo of the previous night's fear.

She took a deep breath and stepped into the room.

She'd been in here that morning, of course, with Officer Peters, but then she had been focused on the details, looking for signs of disturbance or things that were missing. Nothing had been out of place, and as Peters had said, it looked like the intruder had never come upstairs. But now, as she stood and took in the room as a whole, it seemed unaccountably strange and unfamiliar, a room in which some life other than hers was lived. She felt a sudden stab of longing for the safety and security of her bedroom at home in Brookfield, though it was so much smaller than this. Then she heard Alice's voice calling from downstairs.

"Annie? We forgot to pick up garbage bags."

And Annie suddenly remembered that she had good friends here in Stony Point. She stepped out into the hall to call, "There should be some under the kitchen sink," and when she stepped back in, it was into her familiar bedroom in Grey Gables once again.

After another look around the room, she returned to the stairs and climbed to the attic to retrieve a small blue suitcase. She carried this to her bedroom, placed it open on the bed, and began to fill it with clothes from her closet and bureau. And as she did so, a small spark kindled and grew inside her. The sadness she had felt at her temporary sense of dislocation was replaced by anger at the thought that someone had violated her home, threatened her within the bounds of her own sanctum, and that she could do nothing about it.

For a while, she flung clothes about, folding them with

ferocity and shoving them into the suitcase. But after a while, she calmed down and told herself that this response was no more productive than the sadness. She had turned the matter over to the police, and that was the best—the only—thing she could do. They would do their best with it.

She closed and lifted the suitcase from the bed, and on her way out, she stopped once again to survey the room. She was glad she wouldn't be sleeping there tonight, and she admitted to herself that Alice was right: She would probably need several days away. But at least now she could imagine returning to this room, to the normal round of her life there, and she looked forward to it.

She carried the suitcase downstairs and left it standing in the hall. She found Alice at the back of the house in the family room—the room that had been the most disrupted. Books and magazines were strewn about, the cushions pulled from chairs and sofas, and various knickknacks swept from tables and shelves to the floor. As Alice cleaned the various surfaces, Annie moved about the room, restoring furniture and other items to their rightful positions. The glass in a framed photograph was cracked, but fortunately little seemed to be actually broken.

Alice watched her friend with concern for a few moments but relaxed when it seemed that Annie was handling it well. "This can be your spring cleaning," she said. She got a small smile from Annie, but no other response. After a moment, she continued tentatively, "I was thinking, one thing you need to do when we get home, or maybe this evening ..." Annie stopped and looked at her as she paused. "You should call LeeAnn."

Annie frowned. Telling her daughter about the break-in was going to be upsetting for both of them. And the distance was going to make LeeAnn's concern and frustration that much more acute.

"Do you want me to call her?" Alice asked gently.

Annie shook her head. "No, she'll really freak out if she thinks I'm too prostrated even to come to the phone. But you're right," she sighed. "I should call her."

As if on cue, Annie's phone rang. The women looked at one another in surprise, and Alice said, "Maybe that's her."

Annie didn't bother saying that LeeAnn never called at this time of the day; she just went to the phone and answered it. But for several moments, no voice responded to her greeting. "Hello?" she said again, somewhat impatiently.

Finally, a harsh male voice said, "It isn't yours."

Annie blinked in surprise and could think of nothing to say other than "Excuse me?"

"The map, it isn't yours," the voice croaked. It didn't sound like a normal speaking voice; it sounded like someone trying to disguise his voice.

But Annie barely registered this thought, because suddenly the anger that she'd felt upstairs came flooding back. Alice watched in astonishment as Annie's back straightened and her expression hardened.

"Who is this?" she snapped. "What do you want?"

"You must return the map," said the voice.

"Return it? Return it to whom?" She heard a breath drawn in at the other end of the line, but Annie sensed a hesitation. "Are you saying it's yours?" she demanded. "Who are you? If the map is yours, why don't you just come forward and say so? Why all this sneaking about, and breaking and entering?" Annie was all but yelling into the phone now. Alice stood stock still, watching Annie in surprise and distress.

"You should give it back," the voice repeated.

"I don't see that it's yours any more than it's mine," Annie said. "It's a historical artifact, and I've given it to the Historical Society where it belongs. If you think it belongs to you, you can take it up with them and leave me alone." She spat out the last words. After a moment, she asked again, "Who is this?" but even as she said it, the call was disconnected.

Annie stared at the receiver in her hand, trembling with the anger.

15

"And the voice was not at all familiar?" Chief Edwards asked again. Annie wearily shook her head.

After the call, Alice had grabbed Annie's suitcase and hustled her out, as if the intruder might have phoned from just outside the house and was ready to break in again. They had immediately crossed to the parked police cruiser and reported the incident. Officer Peters had radioed in the report, walked them to Alice's house, and then, at Alice's insistence, gone into Annie's house to check on things.

After about an hour, Chief Edwards had arrived to hear about the call. Annie had recounted it in as much detail as she could remember, assisted by Alice, who had at least heard Annie's side of the conversation. "But like I said," she continued, "his voice sounded funny, strained. Like maybe he was trying to disguise it."

"Which would suggest it's a voice you might recognize," Alice said.

The chief didn't respond to this, but he looked thoughtful. After a moment, he said, "Since we know the time the call arrived, the phone company should be able to tell us what number it was made from. That was the only call you received, right?"

Annie's expression became alarmed. "Yes, but that raises the question, how did he know to call when he did?

Is he watching me?" Both she and Alice involuntarily turned their heads toward the window.

Chief Edwards shook his head. "I think it's much more likely that he tried several times until he got you. The phone records will tell us. But in the meantime, as you know, I've got Peters out here," he nodded in the direction of the cruiser parked down the street, "and he knows to keep an eye on both these houses."

After the chief had left, Alice began to prepare the lasagna while Annie called her daughter in Texas.

"A break-in!" LeeAnn exclaimed in alarm, and Annie could hear her son-in-law's voice in the background calling, "What? What's happened?"

"Mother, what is going on up there?"

Trying to keep her voice calm and her tone light, Annie updated LeeAnn on the embroidered map, the efforts to research its history, the Historical Society exhibit, and the consultation with the expert from Boston. She tried to minimize the break-ins at the Cultural Center and at her own house, and she emphasized the allure of the map. LeeAnn was having none of it.

"I knew something was wrong as soon as the phone rang," she said, "and the caller ID showed it was coming from Alice's phone and not yours. I was so relieved to hear your voice when I picked up. But I never dreamed you'd be telling me something like this. Mother, what are you going to do? Do you want us to come up there and stay with you?"

"Well, of course I always like to have you visit," Annie faltered, "but no, you don't need to come rushing up to protect me." If there was any danger, the last thing Annie wanted was to have her daughter or grandchildren mixed up in it. "The police are handling everything," she continued more confidently. "They've got an officer stationed outside the house right now."

"You're under guard?" exclaimed LeeAnn.

"And besides," Annie continued hastily, "Alice has offered to put me up at her house. Just for a couple of nights, you know, while I get over the … surprise."

LeeAnn was silent for a few moments. "So you're staying with Alice?" she finally asked.

"Yes, and she's fixing a lovely supper right now that's intended to help us forget all about this."

"And the police think that's a good idea? Maybe you should go check into a motel or something. Or come down here."

"Chief Edwards thought it was a fine idea." That might be stretching it some, Annie considered, but he certainly hadn't objected.

LeeAnn gave a soft, doubtful grunt. "Well, OK. But I hope the both of you will be very careful. And I want you to call me immediately if anything else happens." She sighed. "Mother, promise you'll call me every day until this gets resolved."

* * * *

The lasagna didn't exactly make Annie forget everything that had happened in the past twenty-four hours, but the soothing food and some chewy Italian bread they'd picked up helped calm her mind and shake off the persistent worry. Alice tried valiantly to make conversation on other topics, but they both found themselves reverting irresistibly to the mystery of the embroidered map and the break-ins.

"If they really are connected," Alice commented more than once. "That's still just a supposition."

Annie shrugged. Her own instinct was that the two matters were very much connected, and she was sure that Alice felt the same, deep down. Alice was just trying to spare Annie further worry.

They'd drifted into a long silence, each musing on the mystery, when Annie suddenly said, "But why Gus St. Pierre?"

Alice immediately understood that she was referring to Hank Page's suspicions. She gave a small laugh. "Oh, those two. They've been at it for years. I think maybe Hank just wishes it were Gus."

"But why?"

Alice shook her head. "I've heard that there's a long history between the families, the Pages and the St. Pierres, but I don't know the story of that. But even if there isn't, Hank and Gus have plenty of history of their own." She thought for a moment. "And I guess 'history' is the operative word. I think it's mostly a matter of professional jealousy, or rivalry.

"Hank's always been pretty active as an amateur historian, even when he was teaching. He developed a reputation as the go-to guy on questions of local history, any time there was an article in the paper or something like that. Everyone in town respected his knowledge.

"Then Gus came along, a younger guy. He didn't have the standing among the locals, but somehow he had the funding for things like his Maine FolkArts Center, and because he had that sort of institutional base, he started to get a reputation as the local expert among people who weren't from around here. And that's kind of where they've stood for a while: Hank has seniority and the respect of Stony Point residents, but people from away don't know who he is. I won't say Gus isn't respected by the locals, but they generally don't think he's as knowledgeable as Hank; plus there's a lingering prejudice against his family. However, he's had much better luck attracting funding and establishing himself with outsiders. Though, of course, that just works against him even more with the locals."

"But you'd think, with their common interests, they'd like each other," Annie protested.

"What's that they say about academics? The feelings run so high because the stakes are so small?" Alice said. "I don't know if they've ever spent enough time together to find out if they'd like each other."

"It just seems like kind of a waste," Annie said, shaking her head. "If they cooperated, they might be able to do even more for the community."

"I don't mean to make it sound like a blood feud. They don't care for each other, but plenty of people, like Liz, can get along with both of them."

After a few moments, Annie said, "What did you mean about a lingering prejudice against Gus's family?"

"Ah. Well ..." Alice hesitated, but she made it a rule to be as forthcoming with Annie as possible about matters of local information. She wasn't much of a gossip, but she understood that people who'd lived for a long time in a community picked up attitudes and information that newer arrivals just weren't privy to. "Gus and his sister have both done pretty well," she said, "but before their generation, the St. Pierres were generally considered to be ne'er-do-wells, 'white trash' as you might say down south." Annie had long since learned that most people in Maine thought Texas might as well have been the heart of the Confederacy.

"That's maybe too harsh," Alice continued. "They certainly weren't as despised as their cousins the Burkes. Now there was a family of good-for-nothings. The St. Pierres weren't that bad, and when they did get into real trouble, it usually came from hanging around with their Burke relations. On the other hand, they had the French Canadian thing working against them because of their name, whereas the Burkes had changed their name."

"The French Canadian thing?"

"Oh, Annie, surely you know that French Canadians were despised for years in northern New England? Of course, nowadays everyone's happy to have the Quebecois come down and spend their money, but there was a time when French Canadian immigrants were really looked down on."

"So it was simple discrimination against the St. Pierres and the Burkes?"

"I wouldn't go that far. The Burkes were definitely bad news, and it had nothing to do with their being French Canadian. But the St. Pierres? They had their problems, but yeah, if their heritage had been different, people probably would have cut them more slack." She grimaced. "The treatment of French Canadians was not Maine's finest hour."

"So the St. Pierres have come up in the world, then," Annie said. "What about the Burkes?"

"The Burkes," said Alice, "have all left the area. Thank goodness."

16

Annie awoke the next morning surprised to find that she had slept well and felt refreshed. She'd gone to bed sure that she would lie awake half the night and then suffer nightmares when she finally fell asleep. In fact, she'd fallen asleep immediately and had slept untroubled through the night. "I must be more resilient than I'd thought," she said to herself. Deep inside she was a little proud of this.

The police cruiser was still parked by her house. She and Alice took out some coffee, which was accepted gratefully. Annie glanced toward Grey Gables but decided not to enter. She felt again, however, the kindling of that anger—that some hooligan should be keeping her out of her own house!

After breakfast, Alice gave her a sly look and said, "Since you're here, I might as well put you to work." So Annie spent the morning helping Alice prepare centerpieces for the annual fundraising dinner for the Stony Point Songbirds, a local women's chorus. Now that winter was done and people were creeping out of their homes once again, many community organizations were stepping up their activities. The annual Songbirds' social was a popular event. The money they raised would help support the chorus as it traveled and performed throughout the Down East area during the summer.

After they'd worked steadily for a few hours, Alice said,

"What do you say? Are you ready to face the public?" And when Annie gave her a questioning look, she said, "How about lunch at The Cup & Saucer?"

Annie hesitated for a moment, and then nodded with a smile.

* * * *

As soon as they stepped through the door, Peggy Carson rushed up and put her hands on Annie's shoulders. "Are you all right?" she asked in a low voice.

Though she had tried to prepare herself for something like this, Annie was still a bit startled. But she managed a warm smile and said in a clear voice, "Yes, Peggy, thank you. I'm fine." Before Peggy could say anything further, Annie stepped forward toward a booth, gesturing at it and saying, "May we?"

"Of course, of course," Peggy said, stepping back. "I'll, uh, I'll get you some coffees, OK?"

As they settled themselves in the booth, Annie could tell that many other eyes were discreetly glancing in her direction, so she tried to appear as cheerful and unconcerned as possible. "Don't worry," Alice said with a smile, "they'll get over it in a moment."

Though she'd long since learned the restaurant's menu, Annie took her time scrutinizing the selections just to give herself something to do. After a few moments, she heard the usual buzz of conversation return to its full level. Though she imagined that some of that talk was now about her, she began to feel more comfortable and relaxed.

Soon she was enjoying her favorite tuna salad sandwich, and though several people stopped by the table to express sympathy or outrage, according to their nature, at the invasion of her home, they did not linger or press for details. Several people referred to the "crime wave" that had struck the town.

As they sat enjoying their lunch, Chief Edwards appeared in the doorway and made his way toward them.

Almost every head in the restaurant turned to watch his progress.

"Alice. Annie." The chief nodded his greetings. "I wonder if I might have a word with you, Annie?"

"Certainly, Chief," Annie said in surprise. "Would you care to sit down? Or we're just finishing up, if you need us to go someplace."

The chief took in the bill and the cash that had been laid down on the table. "Well, if you wouldn't mind coming down the street, that might be best." So they rose and followed him out of the restaurant onto Main Street. He turned to the right, and down beyond the intersection with Maple, Annie could see a police car parked in front of the Cultural Center. Her heart sank.

"Is this about the break-in at Annie's?" Alice was asking.

"Yes and no," the chief replied, and Annie touched her friend's arm and pointed down the street. Seeing the gesture, the chief said, "Yes, I'm afraid so. There's been yet another attempt to steal the map, and this time it was successful."

* * * *

The Historical Society's museum in the Cultural Center was staffed by volunteers on rotation. Most had not been told that the map was being locked in the safe when the museum was closed. Either Liz or Hank would simply show up before it was time to open, and by the time volunteers arrived, the map was already on display. As a result, volunteer Bill Witherell had not fully appreciated the precautions in place to safeguard the map.

Staffing the museum during the hours it was open to the public could be a tedious business, especially early or late in the season when the summer people were not fully in residence. During especially slow times, Bill would sometimes hang a "back in five minutes" sign on the door and walk across the street to the lounge at the Maplehurst Inn or down a block to The Cup & Saucer and get a cup of coffee to go. It had never once caused a problem.

That morning he'd not had a single visitor, and he'd completed his personal tour of the exhibit twice. About ten thirty, he'd found himself nodding over his John LeCarre novel, so he'd put down the book, stood, stretched, and decided that a stroll down to the diner was just what he needed. "I wasn't in there for more than ten minutes," he told Chief Edwards. "And then as I stepped out, I looked down the street and thought I saw someone come out the door here. Well, I knew I'd locked it behind me, and this guy took off walking mighty fast in the other direction. I just had a bad feeling, so I ran back down here and found the door broken open and the case smashed."

"And the map was gone," said the chief.

"The map was gone," Bill Witherell confirmed.

The chief sighed. "What did this man look like? The one you saw coming out the door?"

"Jeez, Chief," said Witherell, "I was a block away." But the chief merely glared at him until he furrowed his brow in concentration. "Well, it was a guy, I'm sure of that. Not very tall, and kinda lean and rangy looking. And he wore a baseball cap—black or dark green, maybe blue … it was hard to tell from that distance."

"You said he was slim—like an athlete?"

"No, no, you know, I couldn't say that for sure. Umm … dark hair under the cap, dark clothes. A black jacket maybe, and jeans."

"Facial hair?" asked Annie, who was standing nearby.

Both the chief and Bill Witherell seemed startled by the question, but after a moment, the latter shook his head. "I couldn't tell you. I think he was looking this way when I first stepped out onto the sidewalk, but he turned right away and walked off in the other direction."

"Where did he go?" the chief asked.

Again Witherell shook his head. "I'd lost sight of him even before I got here. I don't know where he went. And then when I came in and saw the mess, I ran back out, but there was no sign of him."

Chief Edwards made a few more notes. "OK, Bill, thanks. I'm going to need you to write up a statement and bring it down to the station." When Bill Witherell had walked away, Chief Edwards turned to Annie. "Facial hair?"

Annie hesitated and then told him about the goateed man, whom she knew as David Coyne's cousin Lionel.

The chief listened carefully and then asked, "But what

makes you think he's got anything to do with this?"

"Nothing," Annie admitted, "just, you know, the 'lean and rangy' part fit. But mostly, I guess, just because he's a stranger. And because he did that thing."

"Waved at you."

"Not waved. It was, I don't know, more of an ironic salute."

The chief sighed, and she knew he was thinking that her house had just been broken into, and she was probably suspicious of anyone unfamiliar right now. "OK," he said at last. "And you say Mary Beth saw him, too, and David Coyne knows him?"

"According to Laura Coyne, they're cousins," Annie said, adding, "though there has been some tension between them."

"So he's not a stranger to everyone, then. I'll keep this in mind, but let's not jump to conclusions. For the time being, we need to focus on what's happened here."

"I guess there's no question that somebody really has been after the map, eh, Chief?" Alice asked.

Chief Edwards nodded. "It certainly looks that way."

"And at Annie's house too. Wouldn't you say?"

The chief's face assumed a troubled look, but Annie was suddenly flooded with relief. If the intruder had been after the map, and he now had it, he wouldn't be making any further calls at Grey Gables. Annie had not been consciously worrying about this, but she was surprised at how the thought lightened her spirits. "Yes," the chief said reluctantly, "that seems likely. But Annie, please don't relax your vigilance too much. After all, this guy has gone to a lot of effort and taken a number of risks to get this map, and the fact is, we don't know why yet."

17

Despite her protests, Chief Edwards asked Annie to plan to visit the police station the next day. "But I've told you everything I know about the map," Annie said.

Edwards nodded sympathetically. "I know we've been over it, Annie," he said, "but now that the map has actually been stolen, it casts a new light on things. Besides, you don't always know what you know, if you follow me; sometimes more details will come to mind on a second or third telling that may seem trivial but in fact offer some insight into what's happened." He shrugged. "If nothing else, I have a responsibility to the investigation to go over it with you again."

Though she still wished to protest, Annie felt it would be ungracious not to offer whatever help she could. Still, she couldn't help muttering, "Second or third telling? Try twentieth or thirtieth." She gave him a wry smile. "What time would be convenient?"

"Morning would be best. Well, but not too early, because I've got …" His voice trailed off as he thought. Finally, he said, "Could you come at eleven?"

Annie promised to be there, and the chief excused himself and walked on to the Cultural Center to continue his investigation. Annie and Alice turned to walk back down Main Street, where they saw Mary Beth Brock watching them intently from the door of A Stitch in Time. As soon as they saw her, she began to hurry toward them.

"Isn't there some psychological thing," said Annie, "where if you keep telling a story over and over you start to unconsciously pad it with details that might just be your imagination?"

Alice considered this. "Everyone loves a good story," she said. "I guess that's why they ask for 'Just the facts, ma'am.' But I don't think you need to worry, Annie. You've been very careful in your recounting of the events."

"What's happened?" cried Mary Beth as she came bustling up. "Annie, is it true that somebody broke into your house? And what's going on down there?" She nodded her head in the direction of the police gathered in front of the Cultural Center.

"Someone finally succeeded in stealing the map," Alice said, though she knew Annie was doomed to tell her story yet again. "And yes, it's true about Annie's house. Someone broke into Grey Gables. The same someone, if you ask me."

Mary Beth grasped Annie's forearm in consternation and sympathy, and Annie said, "I'm fine. I ran to Alice's house, and really there was no harm done."

"No harm to you," Alice said, "but the house sure was a mess."

Mary Beth shook her head, muttering, "My word. My word." Then she looked up and continued, "Would you like some tea? Do you have time to come into the shop for a few minutes?"

She looked from one to the other, but Alice decided to let Annie respond.

"Tea would be lovely," Annie said.

* * * *

Inside the shop, they found Megan Coyne, who had been knitting socks with Mary Beth when they caught wind of the commotion outside. Unsure what to do, Megan had simply sat and continued to knit when Mary Beth had jumped up and ran out the door to see what was happening.

"Oh, Megan, I'm so sorry," Mary Beth said when she caught sight of the girl. "I just ran off and left you, didn't I? Well, you could have come yourself, you know."

"That's OK," Megan said, shyly peering up. "I just kept going. But I need your help with this." She held up her sock. "I've done the heel flap, but I don't understand the directions on turning the heel."

"Ah. No one understands those directions." Mary Beth immediately plopped back down in the chair beside Megan. "You have to do one to learn how to do it. Let's see ... sock heels require close attention, and I don't know if I can concentrate now."

As Alice moved off to put the water on to boil for the tea, Mary Beth took the needles from Megan and peered at the work. "Very good, but you've gone a little too far. You'll need to unknit a couple of stitches, here, and then we'll be at a good stopping place." She handed the sock back to Megan and bit her lip while Megan slowly, cautiously, made her correction. "You can always undo your mistakes—that's the wonderful thing about knitting. Now then, dear, you know Annie, of course." Annie nodded and smiled at the girl. "And do you know Mrs. MacFarlane?"

"Please, call me Alice." Alice held out her hand. Flustered, Megan dropped her knitting into her lap so she could shake it. "Would you like some tea? Mary Beth seems to only have chamomile at the moment. That's lovely yarn for socks." Alice stretched out her hands to look at Megan's project more closely.

"Yes, please," Megan said meekly. "Thank you."

"I love this variegated mix of midnight blue and teal. It looks like the ocean at night when it's knitted up. Mary Beth is right, you do have a natural talent for knitting."

"I must stock up on tea before the next Hook and Needle Club meeting," Mary Beth said, accepting her cup. "Thank you, Alice. Now, Annie, are you quite sure you're all right?"

"I'm fine, yes. I'm staying with Alice for a few days." Continuing right on, she said, "We missed you when we lunched with your mother the other day, Megan. Did you have a good trip to Boston?" She knew that Mary Beth wouldn't let her leave without telling the story of the break-in, but she thought they first ought to try to put the young Coyne girl more at ease. "You visited your mom's cousin, I think?"

"We call her our Aunt Eileen, but she's really Mom's cousin. Oh yes, we had an awesome time," Megan said with enthusiasm. "We went to the Museum of Science and the Mapparium, and we walked the Freedom Trail, and we went on one of the Duck Boats."

"Mapparium?" Annie asked. "Duck Boat?"

"The Mapparium is way cool," Megan said. "It's like

you're standing at the center of the earth! And it's beautiful."

"It's a giant globe made of glass," Alice explained, "with the countries painted on. You walk inside and look out at the surface. It's like being inside a stained-glass window that's painted as a map."

"I guess there are all kinds of ways of rendering maps," Annie said, thinking of the embroidery.

"But it's not up to date," Megan said earnestly. "It hasn't been updated since it was first made." Annie asked her when that was, but Megan couldn't remember.

"Pre-World War II anyway," said Alice.

"And the Duck Boats? I've heard of duck boots," Annie said with a smile.

"The official footwear of Maine," Alice muttered, but the rest ignored her.

"They're trucks that go in the water," Megan said, laughing at the memory. "They leave from the Museum of Science."

"Amphibious vehicles," said Alice. "They give tours of the city from both land and sea. And they're painted bright yellow. Surely you've seen them driving around Boston?"

"But I've never been to Boston," said Annie, whose experience of New England was largely confined to Maine. "At least, not to do more than pass through on my way up here. I've changed planes at the airport. But when I drove up, I took a wide detour around the city. I've heard the traffic is terrible."

"Oh, you should go," said Megan excitedly. "It's so interesting. There's so much to see and do. I'm going to go back by myself sometime, and Aunt Eileen is going to take me to the things that Martin didn't want to do, like the art museum and the symphony." Her young face glowed with excitement, and Mary Beth smiled at her benevolently.

"You really should go, Annie," Alice said, "just for the history."

"Faneuil Hall, the Old North Church," Mary Beth added.

"OK, OK," Annie said, laughing. "I'll go someday. I forget sometimes how obsessed you New Englanders can be with your history." But the mention of history reminded her of the stolen map and the break-in at Grey Gables, and her laughter died away.

In her enthusiasm describing her trip, Megan had again allowed her knitting to drop into her lap, but now, after Annie had been silent a moment, Mary Beth leaned over, picked it up, and put it back in her hands. "Here, dear," she said, "start picking up the stitches along here with this needle, like I showed you." She tapped one of Megan's needles with one of her own.

Megan looked abashed, and Annie instantly felt guilty for bringing the high spirits down. "I'm sorry," she said. "It's just that this whole thing with the embroidered map gets to be too much sometimes. I mean, yes, it's interesting and beautiful. And for all I know it may even be valuable, though neither Hank Page nor Gus St. Pierre seem to think that it's especially so." She sighed. "So why would anyone be so interested in it? Why run the risk of all these break-ins?"

"And is that what happened at Grey Gables?" Mary Beth asked. "Someone broke in looking for the embroidery?"

Annie turned her palms up in a questioning gesture, but Alice said, "The police seem to think it's the most likely explanation. The map wasn't actually in the house, but it's likely the thief didn't know that. And nothing else was taken, though it looks like the thief fled when Annie woke up and ran out of the house."

Megan's eyes had grown wide. "A thief? Were you scared?"

Annie hesitated a moment, and then said simply, "Yes. Yes, I was."

"But you don't know for sure that he was after the map?" Mary Beth asked.

"Well, and then there was the threatening phone call," Alice said.

"Threatening phone call!" exclaimed Mary Beth, who'd heard nothing of this.

"He didn't actually make a threat," Annie said.

"But he did mention the map," Alice replied.

Mary Beth looked from one to the other with an expression of confusion on her face. Finally, she burst out, "So what has been happening?"

Annie gave a small smile. "I'm sorry, Mary Beth. Here's the story." And she told her about the break-in, the phone call, and the most recent—and finally successful—attempt to steal the map.

"So it's really gone," Mary Beth said, shaking her head. "And the police still have no leads, despite all these attempts. You'd think he'd have left some traces."

"Of course, we don't really know that it's been the same person each time," Annie said thoughtfully, but both Alice and Mary Beth frowned at this excess of caution, and she said, "OK, OK. I was just saying."

"Traces are all well and good," Alice said, "but we're not exactly CSI up here. Chief Edwards does a great job, but we just don't have much call for extensive forensic capabilities."

"And you didn't recognize him?"

Annie shook her head. "It was dark. And I was, well, in a hurry."

They all sat in thoughtful silence for a while. Finally, Megan said, "Is this the map that was on display at the Historical Society?"

Annie looked at her. She'd almost forgotten about the girl's presence as she'd brooded over the mystery of the map's disappearance. She smiled at the girl. "Yes, Megan, that's right. Did you see it?"

Megan nodded. "My dad took us to see it the other day. My teacher had talked about it in class, so Dad said we should go have a look at a piece of history." She paused, and then asked, "Where did it come from?"

"I found it in my grandmother's attic," Annie said. "What did you think of it, Megan? Isn't it beautiful?"

"Oh, yes," the girl agreed, but her mind seemed to be on something else. Annie waited while the girl bit her lower lip. Eventually, Megan said, "So, was your grandmother a bootlegger?"

The three women stared at her in amazement. Megan quickly became self-conscious under their gaze. "I'm sorry!" she said quickly, and looked down to begin knitting furiously.

Annie, Alice, and Mary Beth exchanged glances, quickly reaching a tacit agreement. Mary Beth casually took up her knitting again, and said, "That's OK, dear. But … did you ask Annie if her grandmother had been a bootlegger?"

Rather than answer, Megan just muttered, "I'm sorry," once again, and concentrated even harder on her knitting.

Mary Beth glanced up at Annie, who said, "It's OK, Megan. You just took us by surprise. What made you ask that question?"

Megan looked more dejected than ever and began to lose control of her needles. Mary Beth reached out and gently took them from her hands. "You haven't done anything wrong, Megan," she said quietly. "There's no reason to be upset. Just answer Annie's question: why did you ask that?"

Finally, Megan looked up with a bewildered expression on her face. "But isn't it a bootlegger's map?"

* * * *

It took some time to soothe the girl and convince her that they were not angry with her. They talked of other things and helped her to more tea before coming back to the subject.

"Now then, Megan," Mary Beth said at last, "we're very sorry we upset you. We were just surprised. As you can see, we've heard nothing about it being a bootlegger's map, but it's a very interesting idea. Where did you hear it? Is this something your teacher said when she was talking about it?"

Megan shook her head. "My daddy said it. Well, he said it might be a bootlegger's map. Or he wondered if it was."

"This was after he brought your family to see it?" Megan

nodded. "Dear, can you try to remember exactly what he said? Why he thought it might be that?"

Megan frowned. "It was because of the red Xs."

The three women exchanged glances once again, but more discreetly. "What about the red Xs, Megan?" Annie asked.

"Because of the coves. He said the Xs are right where the calmest coves are. The most secluded. And then he said those are the coves that were used by the bootleggers during … Prohibition. So maybe that's a bootlegger's map!" She paused and then turned to Mary Beth to ask, "What's a bootlegger?"

"Didn't you ask your daddy?" Mary Beth asked.

She nodded. "He said it was a smuggler," she said, suggesting by her tone that the answer had left her no wiser than before.

Annie looked at Alice and Mary Beth. "Rum-running? In Maine?"

Alice simply shrugged, but Mary Beth said, "I've heard tell of it, but I've never given it much thought. But yes, I guess it did happen. I don't know how much, but I guess Hank or Liz would know more about it." She looked thoughtfully at Megan. "And David would certainly know the coves," she added.

"Well, who'd a thunk it?" Alice said.

18

By the time Annie and Alice emerged from A Stitch in Time, the police car was gone from the Cultural Center and the Historical Society museum was locked up.

"Let's plan to look for Hank in the morning," Annie said, "before we see Chief Edwards. I'm sure Mary Beth is right: Whatever the local history of rum-running may be, he'll know what it is. Maybe he'll have some insights that will help the chief." Suddenly she shot Alice an apologetic look. "Or I'll look for him, I mean. Just because I'm staying with you doesn't mean you have to be dragged around everywhere I go."

"Are you kidding?" Alice laughed. "I want to hear about the bootleggers too!"

* * * *

As soon as they entered the Cultural Center the next day, Hank Page hurried over with a concerned expression. "Annie, I'm so sorry about this," he said earnestly. "Liz and I want you to know that the Historical Society takes full responsibility for the loss of the map. I hope you're not too upset?"

"Thank you, Hank. Liz called me last night at Alice's, but there's no question of responsibility. I know that you all took steps to keep the map protected, but it seems that someone was very determined. I'm just glad no one was hurt in the process."

Hank nodded with a look of relief, and then gestured with a rueful expression toward the smashed glass top of the cabinet. "Even the display case was an antique," he said, "though it seems to be unharmed but for the glass, and that can be replaced." Then another thought seemed to strike him. "And of course, you had your own misadventure, thanks to the map. How are you holding up?"

"I'm still staying with Alice for a few days," Annie said, "but I'm fine. Really."

There was an awkward pause; then Hank seemed to recall his manners and invited Annie and Alice to the back for some tea.

"I know Liz keeps tea in here somewhere," he muttered, setting out three mismatched mugs.

"Sit down, Hank," Alice said, taking over. "I'll make the tea. Annie has some information for you."

Hank perked up. "What have you learned?"

"Well, it's about the red Xs," Annie began hesitantly. "Someone has suggested that they might mark certain coves. In fact, you said yourself once that one of them was right on the spot for … Pirate's Cove, was it?" Hank nodded, his face thoughtful. "Well, what if they all mark coves?"

Hank jumped up and began to rummage through the papers piled on the desk in the small back office. As he sifted through an overflowing "out" box, he muttered, "We were so dazzled by the embroidery that we couldn't see the forest for the trees, so to speak. Ah!" Suddenly, he thrust up one fist triumphantly, while the other hand held a printout of the photo he had taken with his cell phone. "Here it is!"

He peered at the printout closely, tracing a finger from one X to the next. Finally, he looked up with a sigh. "Well, I can't say, myself. It certainly sounds plausible. All the Xs seem to be placed along the line where the sea meets the land, but I don't know the coast well enough to say if there's really a cove at each spot. Your informant must be a fisherman or a lobsterman. Or at least an enthusiastic sailor."

Annie paused, hesitant to reveal the source of the information. Finally, she said simply, "Yes, that's right." David had been a fisherman, even if he no longer was.

Hank nodded, as if to accept Annie's unwillingness to reveal her source. He gave her an expectant, sidelong glance, but merely observed, "You know, this map could be accurate enough that it would be possible to test your hypothesis." When Annie looked puzzled, he said, "Take a boat. Go out and try to find these spots. See if there are coves there."

"Do you really think we could?" Annie asked in surprise.

Hank shrugged. "We keep referring to this as a map. We should test out the idea that it could actually be used as one."

Annie realized that, though she had been referring to the embroidery piece as a map, she still considered it primarily a decorative object, not something someone could actually use for purposes of navigation. "I just … never really thought it could be accurate enough."

"I think it is," Hank replied.

"But tell him the other part, Annie," Alice finally burst out impatiently. "About the … you know." Hank smiled and once again turned an expectant gaze toward Annie.

"It's just speculation," she began; then she hesitated and started over. "It's about the coves. They aren't just any coves, it seems, but particularly quiet and secluded ones. In fact, they are apparently just the coves that were used for ... bootlegging." She felt foolish saying it; Prohibition had been so long before her time that the very idea of rum-running seemed quaint and not quite real. On the other hand, she was aware that it had been against the law, and that a lot of time and money had been spent all over the country trying to stop the illegal trade (she couldn't help but think of Eliot Ness and Al Capone). So it had occurred to her that Stony Point residents today might not care to be reminded that such things had once gone on in their area.

Hank, however, was beaming. "Bootlegging," he said, drawing out the word with relish. "Well, now, that is a topic of my research: black-market economies and rural development in Maine." He sat back and steepled his fingers as if about to pontificate on the topic, but then he noticed Annie's look of concern and gave her a kindly smile. "I take it you've heard that the topic might have a personal, or I should say familial, interest for me?"

Annie's mouth gaped open in astonishment. "What?"

Hank pulled up short. "I guess you haven't heard after all. But it's OK," he quickly added in a reassuring tone. He stopped to collect his thoughts for a moment while Annie and Alice both stared at him, dumbfounded. "Yes, I'm afraid my Page ancestors were heavily involved in rum-running during the Prohibition years. My grandfather's brother Hiram was the mastermind, but Granddad was in it, too, though he was adamant about keeping my dad out of it. I thought maybe you'd heard something about that, since you seemed so uncomfortable bringing it up." He cocked an inquisitive eyebrow.

"No," Annie said, "I'd no idea." She glanced at Alice, who said, "Nor had I."

"Yes, well, not that they dirtied their own hands with it, of course. They had other local people who did the actual smuggling. But my family provided the capital, the connections, and the distribution; they were the brains of the operation, and they supplied Canadian spirits for a fair part of Maine, collecting most of the profits and bearing little of the risk. They never personally carried a drop across the border."

"Who did?" Annie felt like he expected her to ask the question.

Hank gave her a lopsided smile. "Oh, any number of local fishermen at one time or another. But most of the midnight boat runs were carried out by the St. Pierres and their cousins the Burkes."

Annie was astonished all over again, but Alice gave a sly smile, as if long-known facts were suddenly seen in a new light. "Well, well," she said.

Hank shrugged. "Yes, the St. Pierres resented being forced to take so much of the risk, but even a fraction of the trade was good money, so they all managed to keep the peace for a while. And old Hiram and my grandfather used other folks as well, of course, and still others operated on their own. There were many locals who weren't regular smugglers but who seized a chance or two if the opportunity happened to come along. And you have to realize that those were hard times for a lot of folks."

Hank shrugged. "I've got no problem admitting my own family's faults, and I even find the whole thing fascinating from a historical perspective, but I can imagine that there are some families around—quite a few maybe—for whom any involvement in smuggling is still a big secret and who wouldn't care to have those days brought into the light once again."

Annie frowned. "You mean like Gus?"

Hank shook his head. "No. To give Gus his due, his own interest in history is too strong for him to cover up something like that. I've heard him talk about it quite openly." He paused and added thoughtfully, "The Burkes might be less pleased to be reminded of it, but there aren't any Burkes around here anymore. And even with the Burkes, everyone knew about their involvement. No, the people most likely to be upset are those whose families were only involved in a small way and who managed to keep it secret at the time."

His face grew thoughtful, as if he were trying to think of families who might fit that description. "I remember my father talking about Pastor Eddy's boat being always at the ready. Now he was a character ..." They fell silent for a moment.

If Hank's family ran the operation, Annie reflected, Hank might have more inside information about who had smuggled and who had not. But before he said anything further, they heard the front door creak and felt a rush of air. Annie and Alice stiffened and looked at Hank with alarm, as if they'd been caught discussing a forbidden topic.

He stood up to investigate just as Liz poked her head in the back office.

"Just me," she said blithely, as she set a tote bag stuffed with handheld tape recorders on the desk.

"What's all this?" Hank inquired, plucking one out and examining it.

"This is for the oral history thing, Hank," Liz said in a reproving tone. He nodded to signal his understanding, and Liz turned to Annie and Alice. "I've just borrowed this equipment from the West Waring library for an oral-history project we'll be doing at one of the summer camps. We have about fifteen kids who have signed up to learn about local history. We're going to set them to gathering and transcribing stories from around Stony Point."

"With these?" Hank turned the cheap recorder over in his hands and popped open the lid to the cavity that held the tape. "You don't think the kids will razz us about antiquated technology? Will they even know what cassette tapes are?"

"They're adolescents at summer camp, Hank," Liz said. "We're hardly going to fit them out with the latest digital recording equipment. Not that the library has the funds to buy that kind of stuff anyway," she added. "We're lucky to have these."

"Most of 'em will probably just use some recording app on their phones," Hank muttered, returning the recorder to the bag.

"That's fine too," Liz replied easily. "Maybe it will stop them complaining about the lack of a signal out at the lake."

"Maybe I'll start carrying around an old candlestick phone in my pocket," Hank said, flashing a grin at Annie and Alice. "That'll be a good lesson for the kids too. How many of them have ever seen one?"

"I'm not sure I have," Alice said, "except in old movies."

"When I was a kid ..." Hank began, but he was interrupted by the sound of the front door opening again.

"Hello?" called a voice, and Liz's face fell immediately. But before she could move, Gus St. Pierre stood in the doorway of the office holding a large black case and a small white bakery box tied with festive ribbon. "Well, hello, everyone," he said, gazing about the room. "I thought I'd only find Liz here." He smiled uncertainly and kept his eyes averted from Hank's. He held out the white box for Liz and said, "A little something for you, my dear."

"Why, Gus, thank you so much!" For a moment, her face lit with pleasure; she showed the others the chocolate strawberry tartlets inside the box. "They look delicious. But, Gus," and she now turned to him with an expression of dismay, "I'm so sorry. It never occurred to me to call and let you know." Gus gave her a puzzled frown and she continued, "The embroidery piece has been stolen!"

* * * *

Gus had arrived by appointment to take his documentary-quality photographs of the map. But in all the excitement following its theft, no one had thought to let him know that it was no longer available to be photographed.

When he was told, Gus cast a brief, suspicious glare in Hank's direction, as if this were some ploy to thwart his photographing the embroidery, but Hank himself looked so crestfallen that Gus gazed at the others in consternation. "Stolen?" he repeated blankly, and it seemed to slowly sink in. "Well, I'm— Well. That's a shame. Do you, do the police, know who did it? I mean, this is a small town. There must be some lead?"

Liz shook her head. "It just happened yesterday. Or I guess I should say that yesterday was the day when the thief was finally successful." They filled Gus in on the other attempts that had been made, and he seemed truly shocked to hear about the break-in at Annie's home. Annie noticed that Hank was watching Gus attentively and with a thoughtful look on his face.

"But this is intolerable," Gus exclaimed when they were done. "Breaking into your house? I'm so glad to hear that you weren't hurt, Annie. But who would go to all this trouble and why? That embroidered map is a wonderful piece, but I don't see why anyone would think it worth this kind of effort."

"That's just what we've been saying ourselves," said Liz.

Hank grimaced and leaned back in his chair. "Unless it embarrasses someone—?" Hank looked directly at Gus.

"What are you suggesting, Hank?" Gus said stiffly.

"He's not making an accusation," Liz said quickly, throwing Hank a sharp glance.

Hank sighed and made a conciliatory gesture with his hands. "No, she's right. I'm not. I'm … sorry." He paused contemplatively before adding, "It's just speculation at this point, but we suspect the map might have been used by local rum-runners."

Gus glared for a moment at Hank, and Annie recalled

what she'd just learned concerning their shared family history on this subject. His expression suggested he suspected some further exploitation of the St. Pierres by the Pages. But after a moment, his eyes grew more thoughtful, and she saw him glance down at the printout of the map that lay on the desk. His expression softened and he gazed into the distance, apparently evaluating this theory against his own knowledge of local history.

After a while, a corner of his mouth lifted slightly, and his reluctant fascination was clear. "Interesting notion," he said slowly. "Do go on."

19

On the dot, Annie and Alice arrived at the office of Stony Point's police department. Small though it was, and not particularly active, it hummed with vibrant energy. A radio cackled in the background, a coffeepot was perking, and the dispatcher-receptionist was busy hammering away at a computer at the corner of the front desk. Annie and Alice looked about the small reception area as they waited for the woman at the desk to notice them.

Just as she raised her head and asked if she could help them, however, Chief Edwards emerged from an office to one side and greeted them. Seeing that her boss had the situation in hand, the receptionist returned to her furious typing.

As the chief ushered them into his office, Alice gestured with her head back toward the front desk. "She's … pretty speedy, isn't she?"

The chief smiled. "I don't think she uses the computer so much as wages combat with it. The funny thing is, she knows more about our software systems than anyone else in the department. Despite her apparent hostility to the equipment, she knows a lot about it."

"Or perhaps because of her hostility," Annie suggested. "Know thy enemy."

He gestured them toward two hard-plastic guest chairs in his office. "I appreciate your coming in. I know you must be getting sick of this business, but now that the … map has actually been stolen, things are more definite than when we were merely speculating. And so it seems to me that I should go over it all with you again, to see if I've been missing anything. Can I get you some coffee or anything?"

They declined, and Annie said, "Do you want me to just tell it to you again, or do you want to ask specific questions?"

"Why don't you tell the story in your way," the chief said. "Start from when you first found the map. If I have questions, I'll ask 'em."

Annie nodded, and once again recounted the Saga of the Map, as she'd begun to think of it, bringing the story all the way up to its theft the previous day. Then she said, "Well, and now we've got some new information for you as well."

The chief raised his eyebrows in surprise, but nodded that she should continue. She described the theory that the Xs marked coves and that there might be some connection to Prohibition-era smuggling, and she repeated what Hank had told them of the era.

The chief nodded thoughtfully for a while, and then said, "So your theory is that someone whose family was involved in smuggling recognized this map and made the connection? And now they've stolen it because they don't want some embarrassing family history to come to light?"

Annie and Alice shifted uncomfortably. "Hank Page also thinks it's possible," Alice said.

"Yes," the chief said slowly, "it's possible. Though I'd like a little more confirmation before I start basing any investigation on it. The idea that the Xs mark certain coves is, so far, just a guess. And the business about a connection to bootlegging is an even bigger leap."

"We're thinking of going out in a boat with Hank to check and see if the Xs really mark coves, and if so, what they're like," Annie offered.

"Well, that would help some, if we could determine that it's really the case. Though even if it is, the connection to the smuggling is still a guess. And then, if somebody's trying to cover up the dirty family linen, well, breaking into homes and the Cultural Center are actions that are going to attract more attention than divert it. You'd almost think they would be better off just waiting for the interest in the map to die off. This business just keeps people talking about it."

"Maybe they panicked," Alice suggested. "People aren't always rational when they're upset."

The chief nodded. "Maybe. But if that's the case, then they've been panicked for a bunch of days now, and they've made multiple attempts to get at this thing." He chewed his lower lip. "I'm not dismissing your theory. At least it hangs together, which is more than my own ideas so far. But there are objections as well. And before I start making a list of everyone whose family was involved in the bootlegging trade—and that could be a longish list—I'd rather see if I can gather some more concrete evidence.

"For instance, we were able to get some fingerprints from that busted display cabinet. The state police are helping us to analyze them now. They may just turn out to belong to people who work at the museum, but I'd like to see if we could get some more solid forensic evidence along those lines before we start chasing after theories."

The two women nodded.

The chief sighed and pushed back from his desk. "Annie, I think the chances of another break-in at your house are pretty small. I can't afford to keep Peters outside the house any longer, but we'll have someone driving by regularly. Are you going to be OK with that?"

"Yes, of course," Annie said stoutly. "You can't devote all your resources to such a slight possibility."

But she was secretly relieved when Alice said, "She can continue to stay with me for a few days, Chief."

Chief Edwards nodded. "That might be best. And Annie, do let me know what you find when you go out to check on those coves."

* * * *

That night, the phone at Alice's rang. It was Hank, who said, "The forecast for tomorrow is particularly fine. Any chance I could interest you ladies in that boating expedition we discussed?"

And so they arrived at quite an early hour at the town docks—not, of course, as early as the professional fishermen, who had long since set out for the day, but early enough that there was very little other traffic stirring. And early enough so the air was still very chill. Despite her insulated Windbreaker, Annie shivered, surprised to find how quickly she'd become accustomed to the warming spring and how quickly she'd put the cold of winter behind her.

"Good morning, good morning!" Hank came bustling up as soon as they stepped onto the quay. "Now this is sailing weather! I hope you've dressed in layers, because it will be pretty warm before we finish for the day." Hank himself was dressed in shorts and boat shoes but seemed to have several layers of shirt, sweatshirt, and jacket protecting his torso. He had powerful-looking binoculars slung around his neck.

"Did you bring sunscreen?" he inquired as he ushered them along. "No matter, we have plenty. Ladies, I'd like you to meet my grandson Thomas. He has agreed to skipper our little expedition. And this is the Pandora. She belongs to my son, Tom's father."

Tom, a good deal taller than his grandfather, was a polite and taciturn young man, who did not seem to share his grandfather's exuberant energy. But he radiated a comforting air of self-possession and competence. After greeting Alice and Annie, he quietly stowed away their day bags on the Pandora, while Hank pointed out the boat's features.

While Tom was busy with ropes and sails, Hank continued chatting away about the weather and the prospects for their trip, until Annie began to wonder what they were waiting for. She had no sooner formed the thought, however, than Hank seemed to spot something over her shoulder and down the quay. In a suddenly lower voice, he said, "I hope you won't mind, but I've invited someone else to join our party." And he stepped up out of the boat to join the newcomer.

Annie and Alice turned as one and were surprised to see Gus St. Pierre. But they both quickly recovered and greeted him as if they'd expected him.

Gus himself seemed a little nervous, as if he were as surprised as they that he'd been invited. And he probably was, Annie thought. But he seemed to be making an effort to put aside any discomfort or suspicion he might feel and make himself agreeable. He was dressed in a somewhat preppier style: khakis, striped polo shirt, and Top Siders. But if he found the chilly air uncomfortable, he gave no indication of it, and he'd probably be warm enough before long, Annie reflected.

"Gus, I don't know if you've ever met my grandson Tom?" Hank was saying.

"I don't think I've had the pleasure," Gus said, holding out his hand. "You'd be William's boy?"

Gus climbed aboard, and Hank said, "I think we're ready to cast off."

* * * *

The boat accommodated the five of them very comfortably, and Annie, who had little experience of sailing, remarked on its size. "Ah well, not so big as all that," Hank said, gesturing around at the numerous craft in the harbor. "And they do get bigger and bigger all the time. Every few years, the summer people seem to go through a new spasm of competition, and suddenly everyone's got a boat that's five or ten feet longer than what they had before. But the Pandora's a worthy little craft."

As Tom motored them out through the boats moored in the harbor, Annie looked back at the docks and the town. "It's such an odd perspective, to see the town from out here," she said, her eyes following the path of the coast road. "It makes the familiar town seem like a stranger."

Hank nodded. "Yes, I always get that feeling as well. It's an odd sensation in general to view the coast from the ocean, I think. I'm sure the people who go out every day are perfectly used to it, but it still strikes me whenever I go out on the water. And I'm impressed by people who can navigate by landmarks on the shore and tell where they are.

"I find I get much the same sensation from going up in a small plane," he added thoughtfully. "That same sense of a familiar landscape made strange, if you were to fly a plane low over Stony Point, say."

"Have you done that?" Annie asked.

"Oh, yes." Hank nodded. "If nothing else, it's a very interesting historical exercise. A little like looking at a map, only better. You get such a feel for the relative locations of towns and roads and such. How the geography shapes human activity: Why towns get built in certain places, things like that. Like this, it's a change in perspective." He sat silently for a while, and the rest of them watched with interest as Tom cut the motor, raised the sails, and set about the business of harnessing the power of the wind to move the boat.

They sat for a while in silence, enjoying the heel and pull of the boat and the gradually strengthening warmth of the morning sun. Hank seemed lost in his own reflections, and Tom was absorbed in sailing the boat. After a while, Gus said to Tom, "So, why the name 'Pandora'?"

Tom smiled. "My mother says it's because when Dad bought the boat, it was like opening a box of trouble."

Hank came out of his reverie with an explosive laugh, and then said in a confidential tone, "I think he just liked the sound of it." Then he looked about their little group with a bright eye. "So, speaking of maps," he said, and reached for a knapsack at his feet. He withdrew the printout of his photograph of the map and a chart of the local coast. "Tommy and I spent some time making comparisons last night," he said, "and so far, so good. This is the most detailed coastal chart available, and it's definitely possible that the Xs line up with coves all up and down the coast. One or two are a little off, but after all, the thing was embroidered by hand. I think you've got to allow a little margin for error. We'll get a better sense of things if we go and actually look at these spots.

"Plus," he continued, "your informant," he glanced at Annie, "apparently says that these aren't just any coves, but rather particularly quiet ones that were ideal for use by bootleggers during Prohibition." Annie nodded, and Gus gave her a keen glance.

But Hank merely continued. "So again, another reason to go and have a look at the coves themselves. As you know, there are a total of ten red Xs on the map. Tommy and I figure that in one day, we can visit these three here." He tapped three of the Xs with his finger.

Seeing Annie frown, Hank added, "Keep in mind that if someone really used this map for bootlegging, the people using it probably weren't going from cove to cove like we are. For any given smuggling run, they probably just picked one cove and off-loaded there. So in that sense, this map is more like a list of possible coves that could be used, but they didn't use each one for every run."

"I wonder how they kept track of which one to use when," Alice said.

"Well, if those arrangements were made orally, we may not be able to tell. But I'm thinking of those numbers that were written on the back with some sort of grease pencil. I'm wondering if they might be notations about specific smuggling runs."

They all continued to pore over the map and the chart for a while, and Hank and Gus each pointed out various geographical features that had particular historical interest. But after a while, they relaxed and enjoyed the sailing, and the talk became more general. Hank and Gus began recounting local stories and family histories, and Annie was gratified to see an easier rapport developing between the two of them as they ranged over topics of mutual interest. From time to time, Alice egged them on with a question.

But after a while, Hank said, "Here we are, going on like a couple of old gossips, dredging up the ancient history of Stony Point. I'm sorry, Annie; this can't be very interesting for you."

"On the contrary," Annie said earnestly. "I find it fascinating. I'm learning so much. I'm afraid I just don't have much to contribute. My grandmother must not have been very interested in local history, because she never talked about this kind of thing with me."

Hank, Gus, and Alice all looked at Annie in astonishment, and then Alice burst out laughing. "Believe me, Annie, nothing that's been said would come as news to Betsy. She knew everything about this community. If she didn't talk with you about it, I think it's because you mostly came up here as a child, and she wouldn't have considered that appropriate. Now that I think of it, she never started talking with me about this kind of stuff until I was an adult."

Hank and Gus were both nodding. Oh yes, they assured her, Betsy knew everything there was to know. "And you always felt that, whatever she told you, she still knew more than she was saying," Hank added thoughtfully. "Many people confided in her, and she honored those confidences. She was happy to exchange news and gossip, but anything that had been said to her privately stayed that way."

"So you used to visit as a child?" Gus asked. "And how are you finding Stony Point now? Are you connecting with the local residents?"

"Oh, yes," said Annie. "Alice here has been a wonderful help, and so have the members of our needlecraft club down at A Stitch in Time."

"And Mary Beth is another person in whom others tend to confide," Hank said. "I understand she's been a big help to the Coynes since their disaster."

Annie nodded. "She's been a rock for them. In fact, she and I are going to their apartment for dinner tomorrow night. They're such nice people, and they've borne up bravely under their troubles."

Gus shook his head. "Poor Davey," he muttered, and Hank cast a sharp glance at the remark.

"That's right," said Hank, "I tend to forget that the two of you are related. Are you still in touch? You all more or less grew up together, didn't you?"

"Related?" Annie said in surprise.

Gus was nodding to Hank. "As Annie says, they're bearing up well. There's a delay in getting their insurance claim settled, which I think is wearing them down. And there's this loathsome persistent rumor that Davey set the fire himself. I'm afraid that if it reaches the ears of the insurance people, no matter how unfounded it is, they may try to withhold coverage."

"Surely there would have to be an investigation and proof offered before they could do that," Hank said with concern.

Gus shrugged his shoulders to indicate the unknowable depths of insurance tyranny. Then he turned to Annie. "Yes, Davey and I are cousins; my father and Davey's mother were siblings. As Hank says, we grew up together, though I'm afraid we don't see each other now with much regularity. But as I think of it, he did mention how supportive you and this Mary Beth have been. She was his neighbor, yes?"

Annie and Alice talked for a while about Mary Beth and the efforts of the Hook and Needle Club to help the Coynes. After a pause, Annie said, "Well, I suppose I should say that it was David who pointed out the business about the coves. And suggested the possible link with bootlegging."

Neither Hank nor Gus registered any surprise, and both nodded gravely. "What, did you know?" Annie demanded.

"No, no," Hank reassured her. "But it had to be somebody like David. It makes perfect sense."

"He knows the coast very well," added Gus, "and he'd be likely to make the rum-running connection." He and Hank shared a small smile.

"Are you saying his family was involved in smuggling as well?" Annie asked in surprise.

Both men burst out laughing. "Oh, yes," they said. "David's family was definitely involved."

The sun was well up and the air was warming quickly when the Pandora dropped its sails and motored into the first of the three small coves they intended to visit. After a very narrow entrance, the cove opened out somewhat, but as Annie looked around its shore, her heart sank. To her left was a largish house. To her right was something that looked like a compound: a main house, multiple outbuildings and sheds, and all mostly enclosed by a perimeter fence. Except at the farthest inland reach of the cove, the trees had been cleared all around.

In the silence, she heard several dogs begin to bark furiously from the compound.

"Look at these houses!" she exclaimed. "This is hardly a quiet, isolated spot."

The others stood gazing around them as she was, except for Gus, who kept looking back and forth between the chart and compound. After a moment, he said, "Is that the Treadwell place?"

"Ah," Hank said softly, and he glanced at his grandson, who nodded his agreement. Hank trained his binoculars on the compound.

"Treadwell ..." Alice said softly, as if trying to recall something.

"As in Jameson Treadwell, the Hollywood producer," Hank said, turning to Annie, handing her the binoculars. "It was a big controversy about ten years ago. He poses publicly as being such a big environmentalist, and then he came out here to build this monstrosity," he gestured at the compound, "and rode roughshod over every environmental concern that was raised—not to mention zoning regulations."

"I see ..." Annie said doubtfully. Through the binoculars, she could make out gardens, a gazebo, well-manicured lawns, a tennis court, and even more discreet little outbuildings than she had seen at first. Some of them looked like small cabins. For guests? Servants? Were they working studios?

"Because before that," Gus explained, "this was all undeveloped land."

"Oh, of course," Annie said, the light dawning.

"A lot of things have changed since the days of Prohibition," Hank said. "A lot of things. We'll have to keep that in mind as we check out these coves. But in this case," he cocked an eyebrow at Gus, "I think it's fair to say we think this cove would have been pretty isolated back in those days."

Gus nodded his agreement.

20

They broke out a picnic lunch while they sailed on to the next cove, Tommy eating while he worked the boat, and Hank putting down his food from time to time to help. Annie had had little experience of the ocean since her girlhood, and she had worried how her adult stomach would respond to being afloat. But though the surface of the water was choppy with the wind that drove their boat, the ocean was calm beneath the superficial froth. Annie had not been bothered by the motion in the slightest, and when the food came out, she was surprised to find herself quite hungry.

The salt air added piquancy to their chicken salad sandwiches, and soon the group was laughing and chatting.

"So where to next?" Alice asked after a while, dabbing at her chin with a cloth napkin.

Tommy responded, "Pirate's Cove. It's the easiest one to navigate in and out of."

"The famous Pirate's Cove," Annie exclaimed, and she looked back and forth between Hank and Gus. "Why is it called that?" Gus had just taken a bite of his sandwich, so he inclined his head to let Hank respond.

"Pretty much for the reason you'd expect," Hank said. "The cove was said to be one used by pirates back in the eighteenth century."

"Were there really pirates in Maine?" asked Alice.

"Of course! Many of those West Indian pirates ranged all up and down the Atlantic seaboard. Why, Blackbeard is said to have buried his treasure down on the Isles of Shoals off of Portsmouth. William Fly, Ned Low, and many others were all active off the Maine coast at one time or another."

"And is there any buried treasure in Pirate's Cove?" asked Alice with a cocked eyebrow.

"Arrr, well, me lassie," Hank began but quickly dropped his attempt to talk like a pirate. "There's always talk of buried treasure anyplace where pirates were active. The thought of one inevitably leads to hopes for the other. So, yes, I've heard it said about Pirate's Cove, but as far as I can tell, there's nothing more to that than relatively modern wishful thinking."

"We don't need pirate treasure," Tommy remarked over his shoulder as he gazed forward. "We have our own hidden-treasure rumors in Stony Point."

For a moment, Hank and Gus looked uneasily at one another and then both relaxed and smiled. But when they didn't speak, Alice demanded, "Well?"

They both hesitated, and then Hank said to Gus, "They're your cousins."

To which Gus quickly retorted, "It was your liquor," and both men laughed. After a moment, Gus said, "He's talking about the so-called Burke Hoard. Actually, this all goes back to your Prohibition-era rum-running."

"I told you how my grandfather was the local organizer of a lot of the smuggling," Hank said, and the two women nodded. "And I mentioned how the Burkes were the ones who did a lot of the actual grunt work?" They nodded again.

"Well, the story is that, toward the end of the Prohibition era, the Burkes stole—" he glanced at Gus, who merely nodded "—a big shipment of that liquor. They told Granddad that they'd been overhauled by the Coast Guard at sea and forced to dump the hooch, but they actually kept it and sold it themselves.

"But it was so much money all at once that spending it would have made their theft obvious, so they buried it someplace. And then the patriarch of the family, the one guy who knew where it was hidden, died without revealing the secret. And so the Burke Hoard, as it's called, is still out there somewhere, waiting for someone to find it and dig it up. Or that's how the story goes."

"It was most likely just old Willard fantasizing," said Gus with a note of disgust in his voice. "Apparently, he was always telling tales like that, and there was no truth to any of them. Each story faded out as he'd go on to a new one, but the Burke Hoard story happened to be his current favorite when he died unexpectedly, and it stuck in a way that his other stories didn't. But there was no more to it than to any of the others."

"Didn't stop people from believing it, though," Hank said.

"That's your wishful thinking again," said Gus. "I'd rather have a pirate story, myself. At least the story about Blackbeard's treasure on the Isles of Shoals has the dignity of antiquity."

Suddenly Annie, who had been gazing past Gus's shoulder out to sea, gave a startled gasp. "My word," she said, "is that a cruise ship?"

The rest all glanced casually in the direction of the enormous vessel. Even though it was quite a bit farther out to sea, it registered as huge. "Certainly," Hank said, a note of puzzlement in his voice. "It's a little early in the season, I guess …"

"But I mean, in Maine?" Annie said, and the others nodded sadly.

"They're like the pirates," Hank said. "They're not just limited to the Caribbean."

"Maine has been the big growth area for the cruise lines over the past few years, Annie," Alice said. "Up the coast and to the maritime provinces. I read recently that where the rest of the industry has been flat, cruises in this area have been the only growing segment of the business. They pass by us, of course, but they'll anchor up in Bar Harbor so people can visit Mount Desert Island."

"I guess I just hadn't thought about it," Annie said with a laugh, but the incident had refocused her attention on the sea surrounding them, and she continued, "It seems like there are more boats around now. I can see several sails." She turned her neck to look all about.

"It's because we're approaching Pirate's Cove," Tommy said over his shoulder. "There's a marina there."

"Of course," Gus said, snapping his fingers. "I have a cousin who keeps her boat there."

As they motored into the cove, they could see the marina at the far end, with numerous sailboats of various sizes coming and going. "So it's the same question as the Treadwell place," Hank said. "Was this here during Prohibition? Or has it been built since?

"We'll have to check," he continued, "but I seem to recall that this was built during the fifties. And doesn't the fact they chose this spot for a marina suggest that it's a nice, sheltered spot?"

* * * *

The third and final cove of the day came much closer to matching Annie's expectations. It was smaller than the other two, but like them, it had a very narrow mouth that opened into a wider pool. There was a small beach at the far end, but otherwise cliffs rose up to forested headlands. The breeze did not make it into the cove, and it was a calm and peaceful spot. After dropping an anchor, they all just sat and looked about for some time.

"Well," said Hank at last. "This is more like it."

Gus was gazing about with a somewhat more critical eye. "It does seem to meet the requirement for peaceful isolation," he said thoughtfully. "So, let's see, how would this work? You bring your boat in here and offload your cargo of liquor onto the beach. And then what? How do you get it up the hill?"

Hank trained his binoculars on the beach. "There is a path," he announced after a few moments. "It's hard to tell, but I don't think it's as steep as these cliffs on the sides." He handed the binoculars to Gus. "It would be work, but I think you could carry your cargo up it. Of course, it also depends on what's at the other end of the path—how close you can get your vehicle so you're not lugging your crates overland. But still, I think it's feasible."

Gus nodded and handed back the binoculars, asking, "But what's going on with the beach?"

Hank refocused and examined the small stretch of beach and the rise above it. "You're right, it's all disturbed somehow. Maybe some animal has been digging down here, though I can't imagine why. And it seems awfully extensive."

Tommy was also studying the beach with his unaided eye. "Maybe somebody's had some equipment down here," he suggested. "Maybe they're trying to grade the beach. Or even expand it."

Hank shrugged, handing the binoculars to Annie. "Yes, probably some attempt to 'improve' the beach. Though I don't know about equipment. The trail doesn't look like anything big has been brought down. At least from here."

Annie studied the small beach, but she could only see the signs of digging that the others had pointed to. Who had done it or why was a mystery.

"All in all," Hank said, "I think our trip today has tended to confirm the theory about the map. The Xs do seem to correspond not just with coves but with a particular kind of cove. They've all been fairly sheltered and not terribly large. And even though some of them have been developed since the thirties, it's at least possible that at that time they were all pretty isolated.

"I'm not sure I'd say the theory is proven yet, but I feel more confident that this," he held up the printout, "is a smuggler's map."

21

When they returned to the harbor, Tommy had to go home to his young family, but the rest repaired to The Cup & Saucer for dinner.

They sat in a booth by the front window, and Annie looked out into the dusk on Main Street. She was suddenly struck by how the days were lengthening, and she smiled to think of the summer coming on. The others had the coastal chart and the printout of the map spread on the table, and Hank was pointing out other corresponding coves that he and Tommy had tentatively identified. The three locals were trying to recall what they knew of each area and whether it was built up, and if so, if it had been done since the Depression, but they weren't having much luck.

"Doesn't the road travel right along the coast through here?" Alice asked, tapping a spot near one of the coves of interest. "And I think there are a number of houses through there now." Hank murmured a distracted agreement, but he was closely studying another spot. Alice sat back in the booth and sighed. "I only know things from the shore side," she said. "Or really, only from the road. I'm sure the coast is riddled with coves I know nothing about, and even though it seems to me that every inch of the Maine seashore has now been built up, that's probably not the case."

"We should consult Davey," Gus said, "or someone

like him. Someone who really knows the coast from the ocean side."

"Yes, that would be wise," Hank said, nodding, "though there's nothing like firsthand observation as well. I think we could make at least one more trip out ourselves, like we did today. Perhaps go down the coast instead of up. If we could visit another three, that would take us to more than half the Xs on the map." He glanced around the table. "If you're up for it," he said brightly.

Then he frowned as he caught sight of Annie. "What's the matter?" he said, quickly concerned. "Annie, what's wrong?"

Annie was frozen in her seat, staring out the window into the rapidly deepening gloom. She'd been idly watching the traffic and pedestrians since her limited coastal knowledge prevented her from contributing to the discussion. But she'd been listening closely and paying little attention to the activity out on Main Street. Suddenly, her eye had been caught by a particular figure, a man passing on the opposite sidewalk. With a start, she'd realized it was Goateed Man. Her companions' voices had faded, and she'd begun to follow him more attentively.

But the shock came a moment later when, somewhere out of sight, the siren of some emergency vehicle had suddenly wailed. The man had jerked, crouched slightly, and frozen for a moment; then he'd recovered himself, glanced about nervously, and started to hurry on. It was just then that Hank had interrupted her thoughts.

"It's him," she said, softly. Then looking at her companions, she continued, "I just saw the man who broke into my house." They immediately all craned their necks toward the window and demanded that she point him out. She did so, though he had almost reached the far end of the block by this time. Without a word, Gus jumped from his seat, ran to the door, and stepped out onto the sidewalk, where he stared intently at the man for a few moments before rejoining the others.

As he sat down, Annie was explaining the glimpse that she'd had of the intruder in her dark living room and how his surprised posture had been the image fixed most indelibly in her mind. "And then, just now, he did it again. Everything was the same. I think even the dim light of the evening helped, because he looked just exactly as he did when I saw him in Grey Gables."

Alice was indignant and pulled out her cell phone to call Chief Edwards immediately, but Hank held up his hand. He hesitated and then said, "Annie, I'm sure you saw something that … reminded you of the break-in, but that's an awfully serious charge. As you've just said yourself, the light is fading fast. And you're essentially making an identification on the basis of a silhouette."

"He's getting away," Alice said in frustration, though in truth, the figure was now completely out of view. After staring intently down the street another moment, she sighed and set her phone on the table. "He's gone."

But Hank was still looking at Annie with an expression of concern on his face. Annie forced herself to stop and think carefully about what Hank had said. She drew a trembling breath. "Yes, Hank, I know it seems tenuous. And I'll be … careful in how I present it to Chief Edwards. But

I am going to tell him. Because for me, it's something much more than just an impression and a silhouette, more than just a similarity of posture. Deep down, I feel sure it was the same man that I saw at Grey Gables." She sat up straight, and her eyes flashed with certainty.

Hank continued to look at her with a doubtful expression on his face, but after a moment, he nodded and looked away. Annie looked around at her other companions. Alice, clearly, had never doubted her friend, and she was ready to go with Annie to the police that moment. But Gus had an odd expression on his face. "You don't believe me?" she asked him.

He gave a small sigh and said, "The problem is, I'm rather afraid that I do." They all looked at him in surprise for a moment, and he added, "The man you just pointed out is my cousin Bucky."

"Bucky?" Hank exclaimed. "Young Lionel?" He twisted in his chair and craned his neck at the window, as if he might still catch a glimpse of the man. "What on earth is he doing here?" he continued, as a turned back to them again.

Gus shrugged. "Who knows? He popped up a few weeks ago at the Folk Arts Center. He tried to claim that Agnes had given him one of her paintings. I didn't believe him, but I loaned him some money myself. Apparently his wife has left him, though I'm not sure why that would bring him back up here."

"But who is he?" Alice demanded, while Annie looked on with keen interest.

"Bucky Burke," said Gus, and Alice and Annie both exclaimed, "Burke?"

Gus continued, "Or Lionel, as he prefers to be called now. We all called him Bucky when we were kids, because his dad was also named Lionel. But the elder Lionel's been dead for years, and Bucky moved away long ago."

"To Massachusetts, wasn't it?" Hank asked.

Gus nodded. "Yes, outside Boston. Worked in construction for a while; then he managed a tattoo parlor, of all things, till the business went bust."

Slowly, Annie said, "So, apparently this Bucky, or Lionel, also knows David Coyne. I've seen them talking together."

Gus gave her an odd look. "Of course he does. We're all cousins; we all grew up together. After Bucky came by the Folk Arts Center, I talked to Davey about him. Apparently he had been staying with the Coynes for a while, until just before the fire, in fact, but then he'd moved on. I think he and Davey may have had words. Davey couldn't understand why Bucky'd come back here, either, but he didn't seem in any hurry to go home."

"So where did he go after he left the Coynes'?" Hank wondered.

Gus looked down at his plate. "We don't know for sure. Agnes has a cabin out on Waring Lake. I doubt she'd have given him permission to use it, but Davey and I figured he'd moved out there anyway once it got warm enough. After the fire, Davey certainly couldn't take him back, and I didn't want him, so we didn't inquire too closely." He grimaced. "I was thinking of calling Agnes to see what she knew about it, but I ... didn't want to stir up trouble.

"To tell you the truth, I almost think she'd rather have him use it without permission. If he asked, she'd be torn between family duty and her knowledge that letting him stay there would be a bad idea. This way, he's taken care of, but she doesn't bear the responsibility."

"Agnes Burke ..." Annie said slowly.

"You saw some of her paintings when you came to the center," Gus reminded her. "She's Bucky's sister. But she's been more successful in life than he has, and it's led to a certain amount of resentment on his part. They hardly speak now, and I think the last time they saw each was probably at my Aunt Yvette's funeral."

"OK, so now he's returned to the area for mysterious reasons," Alice said. "But why on earth would he break into Grey Gables? Why would he want the map? And as far as that goes, how did he even know about it? Annie only found it a few weeks ago, and before that, nobody seems to have known of its existence. Yet here he is, and apparently he went to a lot of effort to steal it."

Hank and Gus looked at one another blankly.

"There was that expert who came up from Boston," Annie said tentatively.

Hank frowned. "I can't imagine what connection she'd have with Lionel Burke," he said slowly. "Nor can I think why she'd be discussing a professional consultation with him."

"Because she knew he came from around here?" suggested Alice. "I mean, if she happened to know him at all, she might make that connection."

But Gus was shaking his head. "The timing's not right. As far as I can recall from what Davey said, Bucky's been in the area since before Annie found the map. Since before the fire, even."

"So it's not the map that brought him up," said Hank. "It was something else. And then he heard about the map, somehow—well, that's reasonable enough. There was a lot of local publicity around the Historical Society exhibit." He glanced sharply at Gus. "Did he say anything to you about the map when he came to see you?"

"No," Gus replied thoughtfully, "and that's a good point. He's not very subtle. If he was interested in the map, I think he would have asked if I'd seen it. And his visit was prior to the exhibit, so he probably had not yet learned of the map's existence."

"And yet, as soon as he did learn of it," Annie said, "it became so important to him that he went to great lengths to get hold of it. Why?"

They all sat in thoughtful silence for a while. "Well, I'll suggest the obvious thing," Alice said. "Maybe he thinks it's valuable, and he can sell it. Maybe down in Boston or someplace else where it wouldn't be recognized."

Hank and Gus glanced at each other and then at Annie. "It's not that the map is without value, either as a decorative object or a historical artifact," Hank said slowly. "But it's not valuable to the degree that would justify this kind of behavior."

"Besides, if he really wanted to sell it, its greatest monetary value would probably be right in this area because of the local interest," Gus added. "The farther away he took it, the harder it would be to find just the right buyer for it."

They sat in silence for a while, interrupted only by a young waitress refilling their coffee cups. Hank drew a pen from his pocket and was idly doodling along the edges of his paper place mat. It was one of the ubiquitous ones with a cartoon rendition of the coast, the same one that helped the women of the Hook and Needle Club conclude that the embroidery piece was indeed a map of sorts.

Lulled by the sound of the pen scratching on the paper, Annie's attention flitted aimlessly through all the events of the past couple of days.

"Hey," she suddenly said, loud enough to draw the waitress back to their table. Annie clasped her hand to her heart and apologized for inadvertently calling her over. When the nervous waitress left, Annie leaned in and said, "We've forgotten about the initials—YSP. Hank, you were wondering if they belonged to one of the two women who ran a trading post around here in the thirties. And now Gus just mentioned his Aunt Yvette. Is that Yvette St. Pierre? Could she be the one who created the map? Might he want it because of the family connection?"

Hank shot Gus a quick look, and Gus nodded at Hank to explain. "My line of thought went bust when I asked Gus about it after the map was stolen—none too diplomatically, I'm sorry to admit."

"Understandable, under the circumstances," Gus said. Turning to Annie and Alice, he explained, "My Aunt Yvette was named for my grandmother's sister, and she and my Grandma Mimi were two mean old cusses. Sharp businesswomen. Mimi—er, Marie to most people—smoked a pipe, about which we all said she wanted to keep her breath on fire so she could scorch anyone who tried to cheat her."

Hank guffawed. "That's no lie. I think my grandfather bore a few of her scars from their time in business together."

"I had wondered about those initials. To be honest, I had hopes of comparing the embroidered map to a few of the handicrafts that are still left in the family to look for points of similarity or even stylistic 'signatures.' It's possible; that line of the family has an artistic streak that Agnes inherited." Gus sipped at his coffee. "Bucky didn't, though, and I doubt he'd feel any sense of ownership if the initials did turn out to be Aunt Yvette's. That's not the Bucky I know."

"But maybe he knows something about the map that you don't," Alice persisted. "Something that would make it more valuable." The two men exchanged another look and shrugged as if to say they found the possibility unlikely.

"Though, really," Annie said slowly, "it doesn't matter what the actual value is. What's important is whether this Lionel believes it's valuable. If he does, that would explain his behavior, even if he's going to be sadly disappointed later." She looked at Gus. "You know him best. Do you think he might believe it?"

Gus appeared stymied for a moment. "I really can't say. I don't know any reason he would think that. But Bucky was never … the brightest bulb in the box. If he had gotten hold of such a notion, I can imagine him becoming a little fixated on it."

"But why the map?" Hank demanded impatiently. "If he's decided to become a burglar, there are surely easier and more valuable things he could steal. Things he could convert much more readily to cash. Why would he be so focused on this map?"

But Gus was still musing on his last comment. "Yes, Bucky could get obsessive sometimes," he said, gazing into space as he remembered. "And he was always susceptible to get-rich-quick schemes of all kinds. That was one of the ways in which Diane—his wife—was really good for him. She was so much more grounded. Without her influence, he'd always be buying lottery tickets or investing in some 'can't-fail' fly-by-night operation." Gus chuckled. "When we were kids, he was always going to find the Burke Hoard and make his fortune that way. I've even heard him talk about it as an adult."

"Good Lord," Annie exclaimed sharply, and they all looked at her in surprise. "Don't you see?" she asked excitedly. "That's what he's doing, that's why he came back to this area. He's looking for the Burke Hoard!"

Annie looked at her companions, her face flushed with excitement and triumph. For a moment, they were all completely silent, and then Hank and Gus burst out laughing at the same moment. They continued for some time.

"What?" Annie finally demanded, a little peevishly. "What's so funny?"

"I'm so sorry," Hank said, trying to stifle his mirth. "Truly, I am. But Annie, there's no such thing as the Burke Hoard. It's just a story. Or at best, a fantastic exaggeration."

Gus looked at him. "Oh? You mean there's something there to exaggerate?"

Hank gestured and cocked his head. "Granddad always maintained there was no full shipment of hooch that had been stolen and sold by the Burkes. But he also said he was pretty sure the Burkes had engaged in a certain amount of skimming: keeping a few bottles of liquor for their own use or to sell privately." He shrugged. "My great-uncle just thought of it as a cost of doing business, part of their compensation. As long as it didn't get out of hand, he turned a blind eye. The Burkes were only going to be selling to their neighbors, not to the big buyers that he dealt with.

"So, yes, the Burkes stole a bit, but there was no stolen shipment leading to a fortune. I'm sure they immediately spent the money they made in their private sales. In fact, my grandfather used to say that was a bit of a problem: The Burkes spent the money they made from the smuggling a little too freely. My great-uncle felt it called attention to them and made people wonder where they got that money during hard times. Or at least, people who didn't already know.

"But I've always assumed it was their private dealing—and the way they spent their money—that gave plausibility to the story of the Burke Hoard. Many folks knew that the Burkes had some liquor and some money, so it was easy enough to believe they had a lot more." Hank shrugged. "Wishful thinking again, perhaps."

Gus was nodding. "Well, that explains some of the things my grandfather used to say. It was his father, Willard, who started the story of the Burke Hoard, and both his widow and my grandmother denied it outright. But Grandfather, especially when he got old, liked to drop little hints about it. He'd never directly confirm the story, but he'd make a show of not fully denying it, either. And he'd make cryptic comments like 'the Burkes got theirs back from the Pages' that he wouldn't explain." He looked at Hank. "I'm thinking now that he was referring to this little side business you've just described."

Hank nodded. "That sounds reasonable."

"But what about young Lionel?" Annie said earnestly. "How did he respond to these cryptic remarks of your grandfather's? You said a minute ago that he dreamed of finding the Burke Hoard."

Gus's face grew troubled. "That's true. He spent much more time with Grandfather than the rest of us, and he loved those stories. And when we were young, he'd talk about finding the Burke Hoard. Well, when we were very young, it was a game we'd all play, like pirates or cowboys and Indians. But as we got older, we used to tease Bucky whenever he started talking about finding the Burke Hoard, and eventually he stopped. I figured he'd outgrown it like the rest of us. Once or twice as an adult, he's mentioned the Burke Hoard, but then he would always pass it off as a kind of joke.

"But I suppose it's possible that he continued to believe the story."

Hank continued to look skeptical. "I don't see how a grown man—" he began, but trailed off.

"People can convince themselves of some pretty outlandish things," Alice said. "And if this Lionel is in financial trouble? The construction industry hasn't been too strong the past couple of years. And apparently his wife has now left him?" Gus nodded. "Well, he could be feeling pretty desperate," she concluded. "And desperate people can do some pretty strange things."

They all considered this for a few moments, until finally Hank said, "But anyway, what has this all got to do with the smuggler's map? We still haven't figured out why he went to so much effort to steal that."

"But don't you see?" Annie said with a sly smile. "Think of how the beach was all dug up at that last cove today." She could see the understanding begin to dawn in their eyes. "He doesn't think it's a smuggler's map," she continued, "or he doesn't think that's all it is. He thinks it's an actual treasure map. He thinks it will help him find the Burke Hoard."

— 22 —

The next morning the four met in the parking lot of the police station and walked in together. Chief Edwards was standing at the desk, talking with the dispatcher who sat on the other side. He held a sheaf of papers in his hands and occasionally peered at them through half-spec reading glasses as he explained something. When he looked up and saw them come trooping in together, he merely raised his eyebrows a bit and ushered them into a small conference room "so we'll have enough chairs."

Once they were seated, Annie's companions all turned toward her. She suddenly felt shy of making her accusation. "Chief Edwards," she began, "I know who the man with the goatee is."

The chief nodded. "Lionel Burke."

"You know?" Annie cried in surprise.

The chief gave her a small smile. "Of course I do. You said this man with the goatee was someone known to David Coyne, so I asked him. Apparently, Mr. Burke has been in the area for weeks." He inclined his head slightly, inviting her to continue.

"The thing is, Chief, I now believe that he's the man who broke into my house."

The chief merely said, "And why is that, Mrs. Dawson?" in a mild tone.

Annie began to recount her experience of the previous evening. Before she'd gone far, she finally penetrated the chief's unflappable demeanor. "You saw him on Main Street? Last night?" the chief exclaimed, and then gave a rueful laugh. "I've been looking for him for two days to talk to him. Well, well. I beg your pardon, Mrs. Dawson; please continue."

So Annie described their experiences and theory, with occasional contributions from the others. The chief, his equilibrium restored, remained silent and attentive throughout. When they were finished, he pursed his lips and sat silently for a moment. "The Burke Hoard," he said, though more thoughtfully than derisively.

But Annie's mind was dwelling on another concern. "Chief Edwards," she said, "Hank has pointed out the ... less than definitive nature of my identification of this Lionel Burke. I had to come to you because I feel quite certain in my own mind of what I say, but at the same time, I must admit the validity of Hank's argument. I would feel terrible if this man's life were ... made difficult because of me, and it turned out he was innocent after all."

The chief gave her a reassuring smile. "Don't worry, Mrs. Dawson. In the police force, we learn to take all the information we get with a grain of salt, even the most unimpeachable eyewitness statements. If Mr. Burke's life ends up being made difficult, it certainly won't happen only on the basis of your say-so.

"But the fact is, I've been wanting to speak with Mr. Burke for a couple of days, and now I want to do so even more." He turned toward Gus. "Has he been in contact with you, Mr. St. Pierre?" Gus nodded and told the story of Burke's visit to the center. "But you've not given him a place to stay, as Mr. Coyne did?" the chief asked. And when Gus said no, he continued, "Any idea where he might be staying?"

Gus hesitated a moment, and then explained about Agnes Burke's cabin on Waring Lake. But he'd hardly finished before the chief was shaking his head. "No, Mr. Coyne told me the same thing, but Burke's not there. Or rather, it seems that he has been there, but he's not now. I had a look in the windows, and there are signs of quite recent occupancy," he hesitated, cocking an eye at Gus to see if he would object to his prying into the cabin, "but every time I've sent someone by, nobody's been home. And that includes the middle of the night last night.

"No, I think he's found somewhere else to stay. Possibly," he added with a grimace, "because I left my card in the door the first time I went out there. I think now maybe I spooked him. Can you think of anywhere else he might go, Mr. St. Pierre? Am I correct that you and Mr. Coyne are the only family that he's got left in the area?"

"Yes," Gus said, "everyone else has moved away. And if he's not at the cabin … maybe he's sleeping in his van? The money I loaned him wouldn't last him long at a motel."

The chief nodded his head. "I've got someone calling around and checking all the roadside motor inns, but we've come up with nothing yet. Well, we'll put that aside for the moment. You've mentioned your trip yesterday to look at these coves. Tell me more about that."

Hank took the lead in describing their examination of the coves and their conclusions that, despite more recent construction, the nature and location of the coves generally supported the theory that the embroidery was a map of smugglers' rendezvous. "Though I guess that's now kind of a moot point," Hank concluded, "if Annie is correct that Lionel Burke stole the map because he thinks it will help him find the Burke Hoard."

The chief completed some notes he'd been taking and then looked up at Annie. "And you think, Mrs. Dawson, that these signs of digging that you saw were evidence that Lionel Burke was looking for his treasure."

"It seemed to make sense to me," she said diffidently.

"So if Burke is also out visiting these coves," the chief said thoughtfully, "how's he going about it? He doesn't have access to a boat as you folks do."

"A boat!" Gus exclaimed. "Yes, of course he does. His sister has a sailboat. Bucky could be using that just as he used her cabin. In fact, well, it's not a huge boat, but it's certainly possible to sleep aboard it. That may be where he went after he left the cabin."

The chief was nodding vigorously. "And where does your cousin keep her boat, Mr. St. Pierre?"

* * * *

Stony Point was a quiet town, hardly a pit of lawlessness, but even so, the chief of police had many responsibilities and demands upon his time. Therefore, it was not until much later in the afternoon that he was able to begin the forty-five minute drive up to Pirate's Cove Marina to see if he could track down Lionel Burke, or at least find out if he'd been using his sister's sailboat.

He could have sent Peters, but he hated to send him so far out of town during his shift, in case he was needed. And he couldn't ask him to go on his own time, though that was just what he was doing himself. It was a bad habit, as his wife constantly pointed out, working off the clock. But Edwards figured that went with being the chief.

At least it was a nice afternoon for a drive. The cruiser purred along up the coast road; in part of his mind, Chief Edwards was happy for the excuse to have the excursion. In a few more weeks, the road would be thick with summer people, but for the moment, there was little traffic, and he could relax. Almost immediately, however, he was frowning again; he sure hoped he could clear up this business about the map before the annual summer influx and all the problems that went with having the population of the town more or less double overnight.

Could Annie Dawson be right that Lionel Burke had stolen the map? She was a level-headed lady, and she seemed very certain. But even she admitted that the conditions for a positive ID from her home invasion were not ideal. On the other hand, Edwards had no problem casting Burke as a suspect. He remembered the man from his previous time in the area. He was not an evil guy, not malicious or cruel, but he did have poor judgment and poor impulse control, and he wasn't the brightest. It was an unfortunate combination of traits that had landed many before him in hot water.

And he was now apparently under some degree of personal stress as well, if his cousins were to be believed. Both David Coyne and Gus St. Pierre had mentioned that Burke's wife had left him and taken their child with her. Something like that was enough to drive smarter men than Bucky Burke to do something stupid. But looking for buried treasure? The chief shook his head. He'd heard vague rumors of the Burke Hoard, but he didn't see how anybody could believe them. Even still, he had put in a call to the police in Burke's town of residence in Massachusetts to see if he could get any information about the man's financial situation.

Lost in thought, the chief almost missed the turn for the road that would take him down to Pirate's Cove. Haven't been down this way in years, he thought to himself. The chief often daydreamed about buying a sailboat himself. He didn't know where he'd find the money to do so, or if he did, when he'd find the time to sail it, but it was a recurring fantasy. He thought that while he was down here, he could check out the marina as a place to keep his own boat someday—when he got it. He smiled at the thought. As he turned to drive in to the marina, he began looking about to get a sense of the place.

Besides, he needed to find someone who could tell him where Agnes Burke's boat was docked.

But even as he was scanning the few buildings, looking for some kind of office, he became aware of a van that was coming in his direction, exiting the marina. Didn't Coyne say that Lionel Burke drove a van? A glance at the tags showed Massachusetts registration, and he looked up at the driver, trying to put a friendly expression on his face.

He found himself looking into eyes wide with panic. Before he could start to wave the driver down, the van heaved slightly and accelerated rapidly toward the exit. Burke took the turn out onto the road so fast, Chief Edwards thought the van might flip over on its side. He performed a rapid Y-turn to reverse direction but then sighed and stopped the cruiser. He'd seen faces with that expression before; giving chase would only cause Burke to run faster and likely would result in an accident. Possibly Burke would only drive himself off the road, but he might instead run headlong into somebody coming from the other direction. Perhaps, without the spur of flashing lights behind him, Burke might be a little less reckless in his flight.

The chief debated for a moment how he could justify roadblocks and how much assistance he might expect from the state police. Then he reached for his radio. Years of practice had allowed him to note and retain the license plate number, and now he called it in and gave the request that set state officers to wait for Burke. He started driving back toward town, traveling at a normal speed but keeping careful watch on the margins for signs that the van had gone off the road.

Whatever else Lionel Burke might or might not have done, he had now clearly fled from the police, and the chief needed to find out why.

23

Annie was nervous about the dinner with the Coynes. Now that she knew who Lionel Burke was, how could she not tell David Coyne that she had accused his cousin of breaking into her house and of later stealing the map?

As they were driving out to the Youngstown Arms, Annie had filled Mary Beth in on all the developments. "I just feel like I'd be in such a false position," Annie said, "accepting their hospitality without telling them this."

Mary Beth frowned. "I don't know, Annie," she said doubtfully. "They've had so much trouble already."

Annie glanced at her friend. "That doesn't sound like the forthright Mary Beth I know," she said. "I think that if you were in my position, it would be the first thing out of your mouth when you walked through the door."

Mary Beth laughed. "Yes, you're probably right," she admitted. "Though that doesn't necessarily mean it's the right thing to do. Much as it pains me to admit it," she added in a facetious tone. "Still," she continued after a moment, "they're going to find out about it eventually, aren't they? It's not like it's going to remain a secret. And so, probably the sooner they know, the better."

Annie nodded. "Yes, but the problem is actually telling them."

Mary Beth reached over and patted her arm. "Just wait for the right moment," she advised. "I'm sure it will come."

* * * *

Laura Coyne greeted them warmly when they arrived. Once again, Annie was struck by the contrast between the current state of the apartment and its dismal atmosphere the first time she had visited. Both children greeted Mary Beth with enthusiasm, and Megan immediately drew Annie into a discussion of several mystery novels she'd recently read. David Coyne smiled genially but said little beyond offering them something to drink.

Soon the conversation was flowing so smoothly that all thoughts of the map and of Lionel Burke retreated to the back of Annie's consciousness. Yet whenever she looked up and saw David gazing benevolently at everyone, she felt again a pang of anxiety; she just wasn't finding an opportunity to broach the subject. She even felt a little surprised that it didn't come up of its own accord; after all, the break-in at the Historical Society and the theft of the map had been one of the chief topics of conversation around town for two days. Then she reflected that the Coynes had plenty of worries without listening to town gossip, and she felt a little ashamed.

After a while, Megan and Mary Beth each had several knitting projects out that they were comparing and showing around. Annie thought she perhaps should try to speak quietly to David about her concerns. Just as she was working up the nerve to do so, however, Laura announced that dinner was served. Everyone else jumped up to go to the table, but Annie sat miserably in her seat. After a moment, the others noticed her, and Megan asked quietly if something was wrong. Annie saw Mary Beth's look of sympathy and took her courage in her hands.

"I'm sorry, folks, but before we eat, I just need to tell you something that concerns, well, a member of your family." Slowly and with much hesitation, she explained her suspicions about Lionel Burke.

"I've only just learned that he is your cousin, David." Despite her nervousness, she kept her eyes fixed on David as she spoke. When she finished, however, she looked around at the rest of the family. The children appeared stunned, but Laura merely seemed sad and concerned, not surprised. Annie brought her gaze back to David, whose face was impassive.

Finally, he said, "Well, if that's true, then I'm very sorry for the trouble my family has caused you, Annie." He paused for another thoughtful moment and then shrugged. "I guess we'll find out in good time." Visibly making an effort to recover his good cheer, he gestured toward the table and asked, "Shall we eat?"

Perhaps inevitably, the conversation continued to be a little strained for some time. But David was clearly determined not to let the news put a damper on the dinner, and the children, recovering quickly from their surprise, were soon once again in high spirits. Laura seemed a bit more subdued, though Annie thought it arose from concern for her husband more than anything else. Annie also made an effort to be a convivial guest, and she felt unburdened now that she had said her piece. After a while everyone relaxed, and the meal flowed smoothly.

They had cleaned their plates and Laura had just mentioned dessert, however, when they suddenly heard the sound of someone pounding up the stairs in the hallway. This was immediately followed by a banging on the apartment door.

David, looking concerned and perplexed, jumped up to open it. He'd no sooner unbolted it than Lionel Burke came pushing his way into the apartment.

"Davey, Davey," he was saying as he entered. "Hey, man, good to see you again. Listen, you gotta help me out, man!" Here he turned and grabbed David by the shoulders. "Please, you gotta loan me your car. Can you do that?"

Stunned, David could only manage a surprised, "My car?"

"Yeah, listen, I'll swap with you, man. No worries, you'll have wheels. You'll have the van. I just wanna trade ..." But even as he was saying this, he finally was looking up and around the apartment. Annie saw him look through the door into the dining room and register the people at the table. "Oh, hi, Laura," he said distractedly, "just a little business with our boy, here. Sorry to interrupt your dinner." But then he did a dramatic double-take as he registered the presence of Annie at the table.

For a few seconds, he stared hard at her; then he tried to recover himself and turned back to David. "So, whaddya say, man? Will you swap with me?"

By this time, Laura was up from the table and moving into the living room, and all the others followed her. David, however, merely gazed at his cousin for a bit and then asked simply, "Why?"

"Oh ... well, ..." Lionel stammered ineffectually. His nervous eyes glanced from David to the others to the door and back to David again. "Uh, you know, just for a change? Variety is the spice, right? And ... and just for a while, if you want. We can switch back, but who knows, man, you might find a van useful. I sure do." This was accompanied by an unconvincing laugh. "But seriously, bro', it's gotta be, like, right now. Whaddya say?" He made a hideous attempt to smile ingratiatingly.

David stood stock-still and continued to gaze levelly at his cousin. Finally, he said, "Lionel, is it true that you were the one who broke into Annie Dawson's house?" He nodded his head in her direction.

Lionel turned to face her directly, and anger flared in his eyes. His pretence of conciliating his cousin vanished. Lunging at Annie, he snarled, "You lie!"

David was quicker, and shoved him across the room so that he landed half-sprawling on the couch. "So it's true," he demanded, advancing on Lionel. "And you were also the one who stole that piece of embroidery? That map?"

Lionel jumped to his feet again and edged away from his cousin. "Davey, Davey," he said, making placating gestures with his hands. "Be cool, man. It's our map, anyway."

But just at that moment, there came more pounding on the apartment door, followed by shouts of "Police! Open up!" David cast a disgusted look at his cousin and turned toward the door. Before he could take a step, however, he was halted by a shrieked, "Stop!" from Lionel. Something in the tone of his voice made everyone turn toward him.

From somewhere under his shirt, Lionel had produced

a bowie knife, and crouching defensively, he now flashed it like a sword at the semicircle of people around him.

"Don't make me use it, man," he said in a soft, pleading voice. David instantly raised his hands and stepped back from the door. In the meantime, the police were pounding once again. "Lionel Burke! We know you're in there! Open up!"

"Go away!" Lionel screamed at the door. "I've got hostages!" Though, in fact, he merely waved the knife at each of them in turn, there was immediately silence on the far side of the door.

"Bucky," David said calmly. "Don't make this worse than it is." He edged slowly toward his cousin. Bucky flashed the knife in David's direction and then back in the direction of Mary Beth and the others.

In a voice with the slightest of tremors, David called out so the police could hear, "He's holding a knife."

After a moment, Chief Edwards's voice came through the door, much quieter and less demanding than before. "Is everyone OK in there? Is anyone hurt?"

"No," David called. "Not yet."

"Mr. Burke," called the chief, "there's no need to do anything rash. We can work this out. If we'll all just remain calm, I'm sure we can come to an understanding." He paused as if inviting a response from Lionel, but the desperate man said nothing and simply stared at the door. The others in the room stood stock-still.

Laura had the kids huddled up close to her. The two youngsters stared wide-eyed at their frantic cousin, more curious and wary, Annie thought, than actually afraid.

"Ah, Lionel?" Laura said softly. "Why don't I take the kids to the bedroom?"

Lionel stared for a moment, blinking rapidly, and Annie wondered if he had understood. But then he nodded assent, and Laura hurried the kids down the hall. As soon as his children were out of the room, David began to take cautious steps toward his cousin.

Panting, Lionel backed away from David's advances until he found himself against the wall. "I just wanted the car, Davey," he said softly, almost to himself. "You let me down. You're family. You're supposed to help me."

"That's right, Bucky," David said. "We are your family, and we want what's best for you. Now, why don't you hand me the knife before you hurt yourself?"

Lionel didn't answer, but unable to keep backing up, he raised the knife and held it out in front of him, grasping it tightly. David stopped moving and spread his hands slowly.

After a moment, the chief tried again. "We can work this out, Lionel. But I need to know what it is you want. Can you tell me what you want, Lionel?"

Lionel wet his lips, his face frozen in an unreadable mask. He opened his mouth and stuttered, "I ... I ...," but so softly that the chief could not have heard it.

After a pause, the chief continued in a coaxing tone, "It's OK, Lionel. Take your time. Just tell me what it is you want. I'm listening."

Finally, Lionel managed to force out a strangled, "Go away! I want you to go away."

There was a beat, and then the chief said, "OK,

Lionel, I hear you. Here's what we're going to do. Me and my men, we're going to go outside, down into the parking lot. Got it? We're going to go away like you said, and you'll be able to see us down there from the window, so you'll know we've done it. And then once we've done that, I'm going to call you on the phone in there, so we can keep talking, and you can tell me what else you want."

There was a sound of feet moving away from the door and down the stairs, but Annie wasn't sure Lionel had even understood what the chief said. Although standing still, David was straining forward as though he wanted to tackle Lionel and grab the knife. But he appeared more worried that Lionel was going to hurt himself than that he would hurt anyone else.

Annie was standing beside Mary Beth, and she could hear her friend's breath coming in quick and shallow gasps. Annie's own heart was thumping in her chest. In the time Lionel had held the dinner party hostage, the night had deepened, but no one turned on the light. Blue and red lights from the cars outside streaked the walls.

But for all the tense anticipation, she nearly jumped out of her skin when the phone rang. And it kept ringing for some time, sounding ominously loud in the silent apartment. Finally, Lionel pointed at Annie with the knife. "Answer it," he said.

Annie took care to move slowly and deliberately to the phone, watching Lionel's face as she picked up the receiver. "Coyne residence," she said in the calmest voice she could muster. "This is Annie Dawson."

There was the slightest hesitation on the other end,

and then Chief Edwards said, "Mrs. Dawson, is anyone hurt up there?"

"No, Chief," she said. "Nobody's hurt." She could see Lionel's eyes flashing dangerously, and she was afraid that if she just answered "yes" or "no" he might get paranoid.

"Does he have a weapon?"

"Yes, Chief. He's got a knife."

"Ask him if he'll get on the line."

She held the receiver away slightly and spoke to Lionel. "The chief asks if you'll get on the line."

Lionel slid along the wall and looked out the window, taking in the commotion below. He wavered for a bit, looking back and forth between Annie and the police down in the parking lot. Finally, he shook his head at her. "He doesn't wish to come to the phone, Chief Edwards," Annie reported.

"OK, Mrs. Dawson, you're doing great. Ask him if he can tell us what he wants." She repeated the question to Lionel, but he just stood there looking from one of them to the next, in turn. So much time passed that the chief finally said, "Mrs. Dawson, are you still there?"

"Still here, Chief. He, uh, seems to be considering the question." Then, holding the receiver out slightly, she said to Lionel, "Are you sure you won't speak to him yourself?"

But Lionel now seemed to be completely paralyzed by indecision, not moving except to wave his knife to remind everyone that he still had a serious weapon in his hand. Breathing quickly, he seemed unable to speak.

The receiver in Annie's outstretched hand began to bark. "Mrs. Dawson? What's going on?"

"It's OK, Chief," she said, quickly pulling back the receiver. "Mr. Burke seems to be considering his options."

Suddenly, Lionel barked, "Hang up the phone!" Annie repeated the instructions to Chief Edwards and then did as she was told.

"Bucky, what do you think is going to happen here?" David now adopted a sterner tone. "Even if you did steal the map, so what? Or break into Annie's house? Those are nothing compared with stabbing someone. Put the knife down and stop this now, and we can work something out. Do you need money?" He paused. When his cousin didn't answer, he asked, "Is it true you're looking for the Burke Hoard?" There were notes of both concern and mockery in his voice.

This was the first thing that seemed to penetrate Lionel's confusion. He started and stared at his cousin. "How did you know that?" he demanded.

David hesitated and then said, "Annie told me."

Lionel once again turned his fury on her. He took a few steps into the center of the room. "You! What business is it of yours? That blasted map didn't belong to you anyway." His movement brought him closer to David, though the latter remained still.

"But Mr. Burke," Annie said in her most reasonable tone, "I always said I would return the map to a legitimate owner if one were to come forward." She instantly regretted this; she had hoped she could defuse the situation by being rational, but she realized she had only emphasized the fact that Lionel himself was not a "legitimate owner." His expression took on a sullen, even angrier, cast. Desperately, she tried to redirect his thinking. "Is there really a Burke Hoard?" she asked. "And no one's found it after all this time?"

"Of course there isn't," David said in a quiet, contemptuous tone, taking a small step forward at the same time.

Lionel was instantly pointing the knife at his cousin, who was almost within reach of its point. "You lie!" he screamed. "Grandpa told me there was. He said it was hidden where no one but a Burke could find it."

"Bucky, don't be ridiculous," David said, inching another step forward. "Grandpa Burke liked to tell stories, just like Great-Grandpa before him. Grandma always said that. You remember." He took another small step as Lionel's arm sagged.

"Then why is there a map?" Lionel demanded. "At first I thought it was somewhere else. But then this map turned up. What else could it be for?"

A cold suspicion crept into Annie's heart. "Mr. Burke," she said quietly. "Before the map came to light, where did you think the money was hidden?"

"Shut up!" He flashed the knife at Annie again. "You shut up now!"

But David had caught the edge in his voice. "Bucky? Where did you think it was?"

Suddenly Lionel looked down at the floor, and the arm holding the knife dropped to his side. "Your house," he muttered.

"At the house?" David repeated. "You were looking for the Burke Hoard at the house? Bucky—" David's voice grew very cold and cutting, "—does this have anything to do with the fire?"

"That was an accident!" Lionel wailed. "I swear it was

an accident. And I warned you. I called you on the phone. I saved your lives!" But he could no longer look in David's direction. With his free hand he pulled up his T-shirt to wipe the sweat from his brow, the hand with the knife still dangling at his side.

In the space of a heartbeat, David rushed forward and grappled with Lionel.

David grabbed Lionel's knife arm in one hand to control it, and with the other hand, he grabbed Lionel's shirtfront in his fist. He swept his right leg around and knocked Lionel's out from under him. In moments, he had Lionel pinned on the floor on his back, his right arm stretched out to the side. For a moment, David's expression was one of unconstrained fury, but he mastered himself, glanced toward Lionel's right hand, and said, "Let go of the knife, Bucky."

When Lionel let the knife slip from his fingers, Annie quickly picked it up and stepped back again, out of reach. Then she circled the figures on the floor to approach the window and gestured to the police below that they should come on up. They charged up the stairs with their guns drawn, but they found the situation in the apartment fully contained, with David pinning his cousin to the floor, Annie awkwardly holding the knife out butt first, Laura sobbing with relief and being comforted by Mary Beth, and the two children peeking out of the bedroom door.

24

"But hadn't this Lionel already left the Coynes' before the fire?" asked Kate Stevens as her crochet needle darted in and out of the project before her.

Both Annie and Mary Beth nodded. Since they'd been among the hostages, they had felt free to press Chief Edwards for more information about the case, and they were now generously sharing their knowledge with their fellow members of the Hook and Needle Club. "Yes," Annie confirmed, "but they'd given him a key to the house in case of emergencies. He was using it to sneak back in at night and poke around in the basement."

"But why did he think this so-called Burke Hoard was even in the house?" asked Gwendolyn. She held her hat project close to her eyes to examine the decreases at the crown.

Mary Beth shrugged. "Process of elimination? Wishful thinking? When he came back to the area, he'd already decided that the treasure had to be in the Coyne house. Apparently as a boy he had looked everyplace else. But it wasn't an unreasonable guess: David's house had been in the Burke family for generations. His grandmother was a Burke, of course, and the house came to David through her."

"How did he manage to start the fire?" asked Peggy.

"That house had only a partial basement," Mary Beth

explained, "and even that was unfinished. Lionel's search had taken him into the crawl space under the rest of the house. Apparently he was deep in there when the bulb burned out in his droplight, leaving him in absolute darkness.

"He had some matches in his pocket, and he was using those to try to find his way out when he somehow managed to set something ablaze. Probably dropped his match, but he says he doesn't know how it happened. Anyway, it seems he panicked. If he'd acted right away, he could have put it out, but he was trapped in a confined space with a fire starting to burn. He managed to scramble out of the crawl space and into the basement, but from there he couldn't reach in effectively to get at the fire.

"In just a few moments, the fire was spreading rapidly. He says he ran up into the house and tried to find an extinguisher or something to carry down water, but I doubt he looked very hard. And soon he decided he needed to get out of there. Once he was out and down the street a ways, he did take out his cell phone and call the house to make sure they were awake and aware of the fire."

"And even after the fire," Annie added, "he was still coming around, trying to see if he could dig in the ruins and keep looking for his lost treasure."

The women in the circle all shook their heads.

"And then he heard about the map," said Stella, rolling her eyes at the absurdity of it all.

"Yes," Annie sighed. "He heard about the map and saw that reproduction of it in the paper. And he apparently came to look at it in person, though the volunteer at the Historical Society didn't know him. He recognized—or thought he did—his great-aunt's initials in the corner, and he may even have seen the map when he was a child. He's been a little cagey about this. He thinks 'maybe' his grandfather may have shown it to him, though neither Gus nor David had ever seen it before, and they all grew up together. We'll probably never know how it came to be in that cookie jar, and Lionel may just be trying to make his actions seem more plausible. The chief thinks so, at any rate."

"He may have been going a little 'round the bend," Mary Beth added. "There are signs that he did some digging at his sister's cabin, too, again looking for the treasure. And that makes no sense, because that's not an old family property. Agnes bought that herself about fifteen years ago."

"But for whatever reason," Annie said, "he became convinced that the map was going to show him the location of the treasure."

"And did he really have permission to use his sister's cabin?" asked Alice.

"Not specifically," Annie said, "but she'd told him in the past that he was welcome to use it whenever he liked. And even though they weren't that close, he did have his own key."

"Didn't the workers at the marina suspect something was up?"

"They'd seen him before with his sister," said Mary Beth. "Plus the hatches on the boat were all locked with padlocks, and he had the keys. That was because the keys were kept in the lake cabin, but to the people at the marina, everything looked fine."

Just then the bell over the door sounded, and Megan

and Laura walked in. Megan was holding two large sheets of poster board folded in half. The ladies of the Hook and Needle Club urged the two to join them in the circle, but Laura stood by while Megan unfolded what turned out to be an oversized thank-you card that she had made with her mother.

"I want to thank you all for the wonderful things you made for us," Laura said to the group. "The day Mary Beth and Annie brought them over was a turning point for us—in so many ways." As her mother spoke, Megan set down the card and opened up the next folded piece of poster board, which this time was an oversized party invitation; it announced a celebration in honor of the Hook and Needle Club members to be held in Mary Beth's shop after hours.

Annie looked over at Mary Beth, who was nodding and beaming with pride at her protégés.

"And I have news to add," Mary Beth said. "On a whim, I drove out to the Two Ewe farm and dropped in on the kids. And guess what?" She paused for dramatic effect. "They aren't exactly kids anymore. Their oldest son just graduated from the University of New Hampshire with a degree in animal husbandry, and they've helped him buy a small farm next door. So they're growing and—I'm going to debut their newest line at the party!"

A twitter rippled through the group, and Mary Beth continued, "And the new line is called …" She held up her hands. "Wait for it …" She grinned. "Four Ewe! Get it?"

The group, including Megan, responded to the pun with laughter and groans, but as the women packed up their projects in their individual tote bags, they were chatting away about the exciting event Mary Beth and Laura had planned for them.

* * * *

When the club's meeting had concluded, Annie and Alice walked down Main Street toward the Cultural Center. Looking toward Magruder's, Annie said, "I still need to stock up on groceries."

"But you must be happy to be back in Grey Gables," Alice said with a smile.

"Alice, I can't thank you enough for putting me up through this," Annie said for only about the hundredth time. "And for helping me get the house back into shape."

"Oh, Annie, you know you don't have to thank me. But are you happy to see the perpetrator now in custody?"

Annie frowned. "I feel a little relief at knowing the whole story," she said, "but Lionel Burke just seems so sad and confused that I can't take any pleasure in seeing him caught. If anything, I hope he'll get some help, but I imagine that he is first going to have to deal with the consequences of his criminal behavior."

They paused outside the door to the Cultural Center. "Well, at least it's nice to see Hank and Gus reconciled," Alice said. Annie smiled and nodded in agreement as she pushed open the door.

Inside, they found both men, along with a woman they didn't recognize. "Annie! Alice!" Hank came hurrying over, smiling broadly. "Here's someone we'd like you to meet." But then he stepped back to let Gus make the introduction.

"This," said Gus, "is my cousin Agnes Burke, Lionel's sister." She was a small, stocky woman who would have been completely unremarkable but for her air of energy and composure.

"Mrs. Dawson," she said, "I am so sorry for the trouble my brother has caused you." They talked for a while of Lionel's status and prospects in court, and then Agnes turned to the embroidered map, which had now been restored to the repaired display case.

"And so this is the famous map," she said. "Gus and Hank were just showing it to me. In fact," she picked up a camera that she had set aside to greet them, "with your permission, I think I'm going to take my own pictures of it." She looked at the map in a considering manner. "I'm not sure yet, but I think I'm going to paint a picture of it."